P9-DMH-396

THE RETAKE

ALSO BY JEN CALONITA

Mirror, Mirror: A Twisted Tale
Conceal, Don't Feel: A Twisted Tale

~

Misfits
Outlaws

~

Flunked
Charmed
Tricked
Switched
Wished
Cursed

~

Turn It Up!

~

VIP: I'm with the Band
VIP: Battle of the Bands

~

Summer State of Mind

~

Belles
Winter White
The Grass Is Always Greener

~

Reality Check

~

Sleepaway Girls

~

Secrets of My Hollywood Life
Secrets of My Hollywood Life: On Location
Secrets of My Hollywood Life: Family Affairs
Secrets of My Hollywood Life: Paparazzi Princess
Secrets of My Hollywood Life: Broadway Lights
Secrets of My Hollywood Life: There's No Place Like Home

THE RETAKE

JEN CALONITA

Delacorte Press

This is a work of fiction. Names, characters, places, and incidents either are the product of the author's imagination or are used fictitiously. Any resemblance to actual persons, living or dead, events, or locales is entirely coincidental.

Text copyright © 2020 by Jen Calonita
Jacket art copyright © 2020 by Liz Dresner

All rights reserved. Published in the United States by Delacorte Press, an imprint of Random House Children's Books, a division of Penguin Random House LLC, New York.

Delacorte Press is a registered trademark and the colophon is a trademark of Penguin Random House LLC.

Visit us on the Web! rhcbooks.com

Educators and librarians, for a variety of teaching tools, visit us at RHTeachersLibrarians.com

Library of Congress Cataloging-in-Publication Data is available upon request.
ISBN 978-0-593-17414-2 (hc) — ISBN 978-0-593-17415-9 (ebook)

The text of this book is set in 11-point Source Serif.
Interior design by Ken Crossland

Printed in Canada
10 9 8 7 6 5 4 3 2 1
First Edition

Random House Children's Books supports the First Amendment and celebrates the right to read.

Penguin Random House LLC supports copyright. Copyright fuels creativity, encourages diverse voices, promotes free speech, and creates a vibrant culture. Thank you for buying an authorized edition of this book and for complying with copyright laws by not reproducing, scanning, or distributing any part in any form without permission. You are supporting writers and allowing Penguin Random House to publish books for every reader.

FOR MY DAD, NICK CALONITA, FOR AGREEING TO BUY ME
MY FAVORITE MOVIE (*BACK TO THE FUTURE*) ON VHS TAPE
EVEN THOUGH IT COST $75 AT THE TIME.
THANKS FOR THE ENDLESS INSPIRATION.

THE RETAKE

CHAPTER ONE

Me: C U @ 5!!!!
Laura: K

I held my cell phone high in the air to get the optimal angle and snapped a photo of me sticking my tongue out. Then I sent it to my best friend, Laura, pleased that the picture was cropped so tight I wouldn't give away my surprise.

Goofy selfies were kind of our thing.

So were creating weird popcorn flavors (jalapeño was a current favorite), putting glitter on everything we owned (including sneaker soles), competing on game nights (I dare anyone to stack a Jenga tower higher than me!), sleeping in my tree house (which we also glittered, but I'm hoping my dad doesn't find out about that renovation), and creating one-of-a-kind birthday surprises for each other (which I was doing right now!). The point is, when you're best friends with someone for six years, you have lots of *things.*

I waited for Laura to send me a selfie back like she always did. Text bubbles appeared in our text message chain, then disappeared. Hmm. . . . Maybe she was busy. I certainly was. Planning the best surprise party ever was hard.

"Okay, I've got the sign up." My older sister, Taryn, was balanced atop a chair barefoot, trying to hang a paper birthday banner for me, but something about it was off.

"You hung it crooked," I pointed out. "The left side is lower than the right."

"No, it's not." Taryn leaned back to admire her handiwork.

"It is!" I took a step back to be sure. The left side was definitely too low. "We need to fix it or the sign will look crooked in all our pictures."

"Zooooeee." Taryn deep-sighed.

Whenever my sister exaggerated my name, I knew she'd had enough of me.

Right then, she'd had enough of me.

"Take your pictures on an angle, then." Taryn jumped down from the chair and shot me a withering look as she adjusted the waistband on her favorite jeans. It was the pair that had just the right number of rips in the legs and that she'd never let me borrow. "I'm not rehanging it. It looks fine."

Fine?

Tonight couldn't be fine. Tonight needed to be epic. Unforgettable. The best celebration in history. You only turned twelve once, and I was determined to make sure Laura never forgot her birthday. Her party banner couldn't be crooked.

But I couldn't tell Taryn that. She rarely hung out with me anymore, and the two of us never talked. She was always out with her friends or on her phone and couldn't be interrupted. The only time I heard from her was when she butted in with a sarcastic comment from two rooms away on whatever conversation I was having. *(Only you would think that, Zoe.)*

I kicked off my flip-flops and climbed onto a bench. "I'll do it myself."

Taryn grabbed her phone off the table. "Knock yourself out, shorty."

I climbed up and stood on my tippy-toes, praying I wouldn't fall. The bench was slightly slippery from the bleach scrubdown we'd given it earlier. I always associated the smell of bleach with the cabanas at Nickerson Beach. My family had shared a bungalow with Laura's family for the past five summers. It wasn't as fancy as it sounded. It was about as big as a shed, the showers were cold, and the one electrical outlet was used to power the minifridge and the toaster, leaving nowhere to charge your cell phone. But I still loved the place. Growing up fifteen minutes from the ocean was one of the perks of living on Long Island. In the summer months Laura and I spent every waking moment at the bungalow together.

But that summer my parents decided we needed some "quality family time." For three weeks they took Taryn and me to every Civil War–battle spot in the South while we lived off the fast-food chains along I-95. Meanwhile, Laura had been here, without me.

Sure, we were still renting the bungalow with Laura's family, but keeping best friends apart for three weeks was just wrong. Once we left, I kept up the texts and calls, but Laura was too busy most days to FaceTime or text me back. And I knew she was legitimately busy. She'd tried out for the community production of *Annie* and scored the part of Molly. Every day while my family and I were on the road, I watched her Snapchats and Insta stories, and it looked like she'd had fun going to pool parties and sleepovers. Sometimes her life looked so amazing, I had to wonder if she was putting on a show for her followers (she had triple the amount I did), but I never brought it up.

Now that I was back, I was determined for us to have real fun, even if it was the first week of August and it felt like summer was basically over. The pool had a weird film on top of it, people started wearing sweatshirts at the beach, and by eight p.m. it was already dark. It was depressing, but I promised to give August a shot. Laura and I still had four weeks, three days, seven hours, and forty-two minutes to make magic happen before seventh grade started. I had so much on my mind and so many questions I'd been storing up to ask her.

Maybe Laura would know what kind of haircut looked good on someone with a round face. I once tried shaggy bangs, like Taylor Swift had at one time, but I didn't wind up looking anything like Taylor. (Maybe part of the problem is that I have thick dark brown hair, not blond.) So I wasn't doing that again.

I also wasn't going to attempt to pick out a first-day-of-school outfit on my own. What did you wear for the first day of seventh grade that looked good, but not like you were trying too hard? True, it was technically the second year of middle school, but sixth grade felt like a dress rehearsal because we only switched classes twice a day. Seventh grade was going to be the real deal, and I was panicked about everything! Like gym. Did people change for gym? *Where* did you change for gym? Did you *have* to change for gym? Last year we didn't have to. We weren't even allowed to try out for middle school sports. In seventh grade we could try out for any team we wanted and had gym three times a week, which made me wonder if we got lockers to keep deodorant in. I didn't want to smell if I had gym first period.

Speaking of lockers, did people decorate them? In sixth grade everyone decorated their lockers, but I wasn't sure if that was the same for seventh grade. Mom showed me a Pinterest board about lockers, with pictures of ones with wallpaper, mirrors, frames, and even a chandelier! It looked cool, but I couldn't decide if this was a mom-cool thing or a seventh-grade-cool thing. Plus, if my locker had all this extra stuff inside, where did I put my books and coat?

And finally, now that we were switching classes every period, and leaving the sixth-grade wing, I felt like I needed a map of Fairview Middle School to navigate the place. Were there any shortcuts around school? What happened if I had first period on the first floor near the gym but second period on the opposite side of school on the second floor? Would I make it there in three minutes without having to barrel people down to get through the crowded halls?

These were some of the fears I hoped Laura and I could figure out together.

But first, we'd have birthday cake.

I tightened the string holding up the left side of the banner, then leaned back to check if it was straight. "*Now* it's perfect." I pulled out my phone and snapped a picture of it. I'd post it after the surprise, along with all the other sure-to-be awesome photos we would take. I just needed to come up with the right hashtag.

Taryn shook her head. "You're so ridiculous. Mom? I'm meeting Avery at the snack shack. Can I have five dollars for pizza?"

"Pizza? We're ordering pizza!" Mom yelled from

somewhere inside the cabana. "Your dad is picking up pies on his way down at around six. Can't you wait to eat?"

Taryn deep-sighed again. "Mooooom, come on."

The two of them were off doing their perfected routine of Mom complaining that Taryn never helped out unless she wanted money, and Taryn whining about how Mom and Dad treated her like a baby when she was almost a sophomore. If this was what was going to happen to Mom and me, I wasn't looking forward to it.

I tuned them out and stared at my (now) perfectly straight banner. HAPPY 12TH BIRTHDAY, OSCAR WINNER LAURA LAN-CASTER! said the red-and-black sign with little gold Oscar statues decorating the border. Even with a 40-percent-off coupon, the banner cost me an entire night's babysitting haul. It was worth it. Laura would flip for the whole Academy Awards vibe I had going on. Red balloons hung from the awning; plastic Oscar statues held down the red table-cloth on the picnic table; and I'd bought Best Actress plates, napkins, and cups for the food and cake, which was also shaped like an Oscar dude. For the final touch, I tacked a Pin-the-Envelope-to-the-Oscar-Winner game on the wall. It was exactly the kind of stupid game Laura and I loved to play. I hoped the party would be a hit.

It had to be, because lately something between Laura and me had felt off.

If I was being completely honest with myself, we'd been

off for a while now. I noticed it the last few months of sixth grade, after she joined the sixth-grade play, but it had gotten worse when summer started. We hadn't been texting twenty-four seven like we always did when we were on vacation, and Laura's Instagram was suddenly filled with pictures of girls I knew only by name. Meanwhile, my feed was all pictures of palm trees and Civil War memorabilia.

When I thought about the way things were with Laura, my stomach felt like it did when my alarm clock didn't go off and I overslept. I was determined to fix things at the party and get Laura and me back to our old selves again.

"Mom, have you heard from Dianne?" I asked.

Dianne is Laura's mom. Some people might think it's weird that I call her by her first name, but I've always called her that. Our moms met when Laura and I were seated at the same table in Ms. LaPolla's first-grade class. Laura sat next to Evan Acker, who picked his nose, and I sat next to Jaden Hempler, who ate glue. Thankfully, Laura and I were across from each other. One day Laura's purple marker ran out in the middle of her drawing a massive rainbow, and I gave her my grape-scented one. The rest is history. We became best friends, and our moms grew close too. They'd only gotten tighter since Laura's parents divorced last winter.

"Zoe, for the tenth time, she's coming after work," Mom said. "And Dianne said Laura is getting a ride down around the same time from some friend from theater camp."

Laura hadn't mentioned who she was getting a ride from, but I guessed that girl would be coming to the party too. At least we had enough food.

Mom dumped a bag of chips into a plastic bowl and placed it on the picnic table next to the other snacks. "Laura thinks you're busy getting your braces on today, remember?"

Yes, and that was a total lie! Dr. Shull, my orthodontist, was putting my braces on the last week of August. Meanwhile, Laura was getting hers off any day now. She'd start seventh grade with straight teeth, and I'd have a mouth full of metal, since my parents wouldn't let me get Invisalign. (Just because Taryn had lost three sets of expensive trays didn't mean I would.)

"Okay. I'm just triple-checking you didn't slip," I stressed. "Because you and Dianne tell each other *everything*."

"Like you and Laura?" Mom gave me the same look Taryn had. Now I knew where Taryn got it from. "Your secret is safe—if you catch the other party guests at the gate before Laura arrives and sees them."

She had a point. "I'm off!" I zipped up my Montauk sweatshirt (Laura and I had bought matching ones when our families vacationed there last summer), slipped on my floral flip-flops, and headed for the west gate. I was halfway down the row of cabanas when I heard someone shouting.

"Duck!"

I did as I was told, just in time to see a fluorescent

yellow lacrosse ball fly over my head and bounce off a SEAS THE DAY sign on the cabana next to me.

A boy scooped the ball up in his lacrosse stick. "Sorry about that," he said.

It was Jake Graser. *The* Jake Graser. The one Laura had been obsessed with ever since he stood up and read some heartfelt poem about sea air in sixth-grade English.

"Didn't mean to get your heart pumping, even if a little adrenaline rush is good for the soul." Jake grinned, showing off braces with blue and orange bands, which were not the kind of colors I'd want in my mouth. Laura thought it was a cute choice since those were his lacrosse team colors.

"I prefer to get my adrenaline rushes from roller coasters," I said. It was one thing Laura and I did not have in common. She hated most amusement park rides, while I lived for them.

"Same." Jake planted his stick in the sand, ball still in the pocket. "You ever been on Skyrush at Hersheypark? The first drop is killer."

"I know, right? I waited for a front car and—" I stopped midsentence. Shouldn't I somehow have been turning this into a conversation about Laura? What better birthday gift could I give her than Jake Graser coming by the cabana for her party? But was it weird to invite a boy to a birthday party for a girl he didn't really know? "Listen. It's Laura Lancaster's—"

"Jake! Manhunt starting now!" someone shouted.

"Coming!" he yelled, and picked up his stick. "I have to go. Bye, Zoe!"

He knew my name? That meant he probably knew Laura's, too. "Bye!" I yelled. "Hey! If you're still here later, come by my cabana!" I wasn't sure he heard me, though. He'd already rounded the corner. My phone buzzed, and I pulled it out of my pocket.

Reagan: Drawbridge is up! Jada and I will be late. Sry!

Unknown Number: Hey. It's Clare. Drawbridge up. Will be late!

For years Laura and I only hung out with each other. But a party with just two people is lame, which is why I invited Reagan Donahue, Jada Reddy, and Clare Stelton. We met Reagan and Jada in Future City, a STEM club we got involved with in sixth grade when our moms insisted we join something. We whined about it at first, but the truth was, I actually really liked it. Not only did you get to imagine, research, and design new cities, you got to come up with ways to solve real problems, like finding places for urban agriculture. Everyone had different ideas. Reagan, who spent all her time playing volleyball and lacrosse and running track, wanted to make sure there were a lot of green spaces for kids to get outside and move. And Jada, who was on a competition dance team, loved creating areas where people could congregate and come together for concerts.

Even though Reagan and Jada seemed like opposites, they were actually best friends who did everything together, kind of like Laura and me.

Clare Stelton wasn't in Future City, but she played volleyball with our team last fall. I say *our* team, but Laura quit after two weeks. Still, she seemed to like Clare, and I did, too, even if she was kind of quiet.

But if all three girls were running late, I had to figure out how to keep Laura away from the cabana so we didn't ruin the surprise.

"Zoeeee!" I saw Taryn frantically waving me over to her and her friend Avery, who were headed toward me with their drinks. "What are you doing walking around? Laura is here already!"

My stomach dropped. "Where? The other girls are stuck at the drawbridge, and you know that takes forever!" I looked around, unsure what to do. "Do I hide? Yell 'surprise'? I don't want her to know about her party till everyone arrives."

Taryn slurped her slushie. It made that noise it makes when there's still a ton of ice and you're sad there is no more syrup. "I think she already knows about it. We just saw her wearing a birthday crown while playing manhunt. Does Mom know how many girls you actually invited? I hope Dad ordered enough pizza."

Taryn wasn't making sense. "Only three people are coming and no one is here yet. You must have seen someone else. Laura's friend isn't dropping her off till five." I looked at my watch. It was only four-thirty. I wish I knew who Laura's friend was. I could have texted her to coordinate the surprise.

"I'm telling you she's already here." Taryn turned me around. "Look! That's her!"

A group of girls I didn't know ran by the row of bungalows we were in, oblivious to us standing there. My stomach lurched. Taryn was right: one of those girls was Laura, and she was wearing a birthday crown I hadn't bought.

Turned out Laura was already at the beach celebrating her birthday.

She just hadn't invited me to join her.

CHAPTER TWO

"Are you *sure* you two are supposed to hang out today?"
Taryn asked as we flattened ourselves against a cabana
so Laura didn't see us gawking. "Because if you ask me, it
looks like someone else threw her a party."

We had plans today. Didn't we? I tried to think back to
the last time we'd actually spoken. It had been a few days.
But we had texted yesterday and today, and both times I
distinctly remembered reminding her about the cabana."
And both times she'd written back "K." How could she
have forgotten so quickly?

I watched as Laura ducked behind a pool lifeguard cabana with the other girls to hide. The sound of her uncontrol-
lable laughter felt like a punch to the gut. The truth was clear:
Laura was having so much fun with her other friends that
she didn't want to leave them and come hang out with me.

I knew I should turn away, but I couldn't. I watched as

the dark-haired girl next to Laura reached over and stole her birthday crown. I recognized her from Laura's latest posts. Her name was Sarah Barden (or @sarahslitlife, as Laura always tagged her). They, and the other girls Laura was with, met during the middle school musical, and they'd also all done *Annie* together.

Laura had wanted me to try out, too, but the thought of getting on a stage paralyzed me with fear. It didn't help that Laura was always telling me how competitive everyone was, and the tears that followed if someone's lines were cut. I didn't want to deal with that stress. There seemed to be so much drama with the play that I secretly dubbed the girls "drama queens"—not that I'd ever tell Laura that. But now, seeing Sarah and Laura looking so happy together with the other girls made me wonder. Had skipping the musical been a mistake?

My phone pinged and I looked down.

Laura: Cabana tomorrow instead? Still out w/friends from Annie. Sry!

"You've got to be kidding me," Taryn said, reading over my shoulder. I quickly pulled my phone away and put it in my pocket, but it was too late. "She *did* ditch you! That's so cold! Why wouldn't she just invite you to hang out with her? They obviously threw her a birthday party too. Shouldn't her so-called best friend be invited to it?"

Avery shook her head. "That's so wrong."

"I never liked that girl," Taryn told Avery. "Laura always had to be in control of everything they did together. If Laura didn't like the idea, they didn't do it. Every time."

I tried to ignore Taryn, but it was hard to do when everything she said seemed right. Laura and I made these plans days ago. If her plans had changed, why hadn't she just told me? Or invited me to hang with the others? I mean, sure, the party I spent all week planning would still be ruined, but at least I wouldn't be standing here watching them with my heart in my throat.

Why hadn't I done the stupid school play?

Why had my parents made me trudge across hot battlefields for three weeks when I could have been here with Laura? She wouldn't be hanging out with Sarah and the drama queens if I had been here the whole time.

"Look at her feed!" Taryn said, nudging me to see the images on her phone. "She's been with these girls all day. Haven't you looked at your Insta?"

"No." I felt foolish as I pulled my phone out of my pocket. "I was busy getting ready for the party."

I knew I should swipe Instagram off my screen, but instead my finger hovered over Laura's stories. *Don't click, Zoe. Don't click!*

I clicked.

Laura's story told me she'd been at the cabanas all day.

There she was with the drama queens doing handstands at the beach! Playing volleyball! Having an ice cream taste test at the snack shack!

I heard the girls' laughter again, and my stomach churned. "Let's just go, okay? Before she sees us." I hurried away, hoping my flip-flops didn't make too much noise.

"Zoe . . . ," Taryn started.

"I want to go," I said louder than I intended.

"Zoe?" Mom came around the corner, saw me, and frowned. "I thought I just saw Laura. Did you already surprise her?"

"Laura ditched her," Taryn blurted out. "She just texted she can't hang because she's already here with other girls who threw her a party. And they didn't invite Zoe."

"Enough, Taryn!" I barked.

Mom looked at me worriedly. "Oh, honey, don't get upset."

"I'm not upset," I said, but my voice suddenly sounded shaky, and all their staring made me feel worse.

"Are you *sure* Laura knew you were getting together today? Because sometimes you say you tell me something and . . ."

I wanted to bury myself in the sand. *I will not cry. I am going to cry. I'm crying.* I wiped the tears on the back of my arm, getting sunscreen in my eyes. *Ouch, ouch, ouch!*

"I'm sure it's just a misunderstanding." Mom's soothing

voice only made me want to cry harder. "Let me call Dianne."

"No! Don't call her mom!" I didn't want Laura finding out I'd been here planning a lame party when she was already at one with girls she clearly liked more than me.

"There you are!"

As if things couldn't get any worse, Dianne was walking toward us, with cupcakes and balloons. Laura's seven-year-old twin sisters, Petra and Paige, trailed behind her. "Where's Laura? Did we miss the surprise? I tried calling, but no one answered their phones." She took one look at my face and frowned. "What's wrong?"

Mom gave me a quick glance and took the cupcakes from Dianne. "These look great! Walk with me a second?"

"Mom, please don't," I begged, but it was too late.

They started walking toward our cabana, and I knew Mom was telling her everything. Dianne looked back at me, then at my mom again. She clutched her chest, and my cheeks burned. My best friend's mom felt sorry for me, and that made me feel worse. I watched Dianne storm off.

"I just want to go home," I told Taryn.

"But aren't your other friends on their way?" Avery asked.

"I'll text them not to come." I stopped when I heard Laura laughing again. When I looked up, she and Sarah were making faces as Laura snapped a picture. Seconds later I got an alert on my phone. So did Taryn. I clicked on the update, and there was a post.

lauraslitlife: Come find us! @sarahslitlife #bestbeachdayEVER #manhunt #nickersoncabanas

"First she breaks plans with you, and then she has the nerve to post about her other plans?" Taryn ranted. "Not cool."

"And look." Avery pointed to the post on Taryn's phone. "They have the same Insta handles—lit life. 'Best beach day ever'? It's not even eighty degrees."

"Ridiculous," Taryn agreed.

"They're in there! Get them!" I heard Jake shout and remembered he was part of the manhunt too. There were more loud shrieks and laughter as the drama queens came tumbling out of the lifeguard shack and ran in different directions. Sarah grabbed Laura's hand, and they started running. Unfortunately, they were headed straight right for us.

There was nowhere to hide. Laura saw me at the same time her mom saw her.

"Zoe!" Laura said in surprise, stopping short.

"Laura!" Dianne marched across the sand, kicking it up as she walked. "I need to talk to you immediately."

Laura dropped Sarah's hand. "Mom? Zoe?" She blinked

hard. "I— Zoe, I didn't know you were already here." She talked fast.

"It's okay." I twisted my rope bracelet around absent-mindedly. Laura and I always got new ones every Memorial Day weekend and wore them all summer till the white turned gray and the rope fit to our wrists. I noticed Laura no longer had hers on.

"No, it's not," Taryn mumbled.

Laura pushed her blond hair behind her ears like she did when she was nervous. "You see, my friends from *Annie* threw me a party. I would have invited you, but . . ."

"You didn't," Taryn chirped.

"Zoe has a surprise for you too," Dianne said before I could even reply. She was smiling, but I could tell from her eerily calm voice she was mad. This was exactly how she sounded when we drank her last seltzer and she claimed she wasn't upset, but Laura and I both knew she was. "That's why I texted you twice—*twice*—today, reminding you to be here at five to meet Zoe. I asked your father to bring you, but he had plans, so you said you'd get a ride. You promised you'd meet me here. *Promised*."

I winced. Dianne was only making things more awkward. The drama queens were all crowding around to listen.

Laura rushed forward. "Mom, I am here. Okay? I'm sorry." She looked at me, her cheeks flushing. "I didn't know you had a surprise for me, Zo-Zo. If I had, I wouldn't have canceled plans."

"You canceled on her?" Her mom sounded shrill.

My face grew hotter. I glanced quickly at her friends, feeling embarrassed. "It's okay. I can show you later," I said at the same time Dianne said, "All of you come with me to the cabana right now."

None of us was about to argue. We followed Dianne down the concrete walkway in a single file. My heart was pounding hard. I couldn't help thinking they'd all find my Oscar decorations babyish.

"Who is she?" I heard one of the drama queens whisper.

"I think it's her friend Zelena."

It's Zoe. I wondered if I could still cut and run.

"It might be Zara. Or is it Zoe?" asked Ava Sinclair, who I knew from school was their group's unofficial leader. Ava had to know who I was. It wasn't like my best friend wouldn't mention me at least once all summer. Right?

"Surprise!" Mom shouted as we arrived.

"Surprise!" yelled Laura's little sisters.

"Happy birthday to YOUUUU!" sang my dad off-key as he came around the corner carrying a stack of pizzas. I definitely wanted to bail now.

Someone read my banner out loud: "'Happy twelfth birthday, Oscar winner Laura Lancaster!'"

I cringed. My whole party felt silly now that the drama

queens were standing here. "Reagan, Jada, and Clare are on their way, but the drawbridge is up. . . ." I closed my eyes and wished harder than I've ever wished for anything to just disappear.

"Oh." Laura shifted uncomfortably and looked at Sarah. Dianne cleared her throat. "This is really nice, Zoe. I—"

But what could she say? *This party is lame? I've found new friends? We don't even hang out anymore?* I didn't want to hear it. I just wanted to leave as much as she did.

"Let's get a picture of all of you together!" Dianne suggested.

She grabbed my hand and Laura's and stood us side by side. The others crowded around awkwardly. Laura and I didn't look at each other. This was not the picture I had envisioned posting on Instagram.

Dianne held up her phone. "Say happy birthday!"

"Happy birthday," everyone said, but there was no heart in it.

Taryn and Avery looked at me as the flash went off and I had a feeling they were thinking the same thing I was.

Laura's summer wasn't just starting, like mine was. She'd already had a full one.

Without me.

CHAPTER THREE

lauraslitlife: Fairview—Lets do this! We're ready!
#firstdayofschool #firstdaybestday

I stared at Laura's latest Instagram post. She and all the drama queens were standing in front of Bagel Boss holding tie-dyed bagels that matched their skirts.

I wasn't sure what surprised me more—their coordinating skirts (which Laura did a whole Insta story on, along with a story on # firstdayblowouts) or the fact that she got up early to get a bagel before the first day of school.

Laura hated alarm clocks! She was late for an appointment to get her braces off!

Who prolongs getting their braces off?

Or posts four times a day?

Not that I was stalking her feed or anything.

Or pining for Laura. If anything, I tried very hard *not* to think about Laura and the Birthday Party Disaster. Or my ex–best friend. It was obvious. I had clearly been demoted from BFF.

I waited for Laura to apologize about what happened. To explain to me that there was some huge misunderstanding that she couldn't tell me about in front of her mom. Instead, she'd basically disappeared from my existence.

I didn't understand what I'd done wrong. One minute Laura and I had been crying and hugging right before I left for vacation, and the next she was ghosting me. My finger hovered over my messages. The last reply from Laura was more than a week ago, and we'd talked only because I'd sent her a text. She hadn't texted me since then. Despite everything I still really missed her. That settled it. I'd send her a short text and see what happened.

Me: First day! Good luck!

I saw the text bubbles pop up right away, and my heart began to soar. Maybe she missed me too.

Laura: ☺☺☺

Not "Let's meet at our lockers before first period so we don't get lost."

Not "What are you wearing today?"

Not "Where do you want to meet for lunch?"

Not "I think we have three periods together, including math." (I only knew that because I overheard Mom talking to Dianne on the phone.)

Not "I miss you."

Just some happy-face emojis.

It was official: We weren't just ex–best friends. We didn't seem to be friends anymore at all. I felt the bile rising in my throat. Was I going to throw up? I couldn't. This was the only outfit I liked, and I only liked it because the girl at the mall said I looked cute in it.

"MOM! I can't find my round brush! Have you seen it?" Taryn shouted.

"It's wherever you left it last, Taryn," Mom called back.

I hated when Mom said that. If Taryn knew where her brush was, why would she ask?

Taryn had done the whole middle school thing already and survived. She'd even managed to navigate high school without any tears. *What is her secret?* I wondered. I peeked out into the hallway and stared at Taryn. She looked effortless standing at the top of the stairs in green jeans and a black tee she had knotted to one side. If anyone could help me survive day one, it was Taryn.

"Mom! I don't remember where I left it! That's why I'm asking you!"

"It didn't walk away, Taryn. Look harder."

"But the bus is coming in ten minutes and my hair is frizzing! Remember the bus? That smelly yellow thing Zoe and I have to take now that you're teaching again full-time?"

Taryn's light brown hair looked perfect to me. It was even curled at the ends like it had been professionally blown out. "Taryn?" I said hesitantly. "You can use my brush. It's in the top drawer."

Taryn eyed me skeptically and reached for my round brush. "Thanks. You wearing that to school?"

I looked down at my navy-blue tee and white jeans self-consciously, hoping there wasn't a mud stain on my pants. I was so nervous about school I'd gotten up early to work on a Future City project. Ms. Pepper, our Future City advisor, had posted on our club board last night that we might want to start thinking about clean water. So this morning I tried making a dirty-water filter using two-liter soda bottles, some mud, and water, and things had gotten a bit out of hand. The muddy water I'd used for the filter had dripped all over the carpet, and I'd tried to clean it up before Mom popped in my room and saw.

"Yes. Does it look okay?"

Taryn turned on the hair dryer and rolled her bangs around my brush. I could barely hear her over the noise. "Yeah, just don't . . ."

"Don't what?" I shouted, pulling at my tee. Was it too short? Too baggy? Were the jeans wrong? Did my new braces make my face look rounder? What was it? *What?*

"Taryn! Three minutes till your bus!" Mom shouted.

Taryn dropped the brush and the blow-dryer. "Enjoy seventh grade." She laughed in a mad-scientist kind of way that made me think she knew I wouldn't.

"Zoe! Come eat something!" Mom yelled from the kitchen.

"Mooooom." Now I sounded like Taryn.

I ran downstairs and found Mom ready to walk out the door. The kitchen table was littered with dishes. Dad left an hour earlier than Mom to teach social studies at a high school thirty-five minutes away, while Mom taught at an elementary school right in our district. Usually, no one cleaned up breakfast till after school. Mom offered me a bagel.

"It's too hard with my braces," I grumbled. I missed bagels so bad already, and it had only been a week.

Mom offered me a peach instead. "This is softer."

True, but not appealing. I was too nervous to eat.

"Zoe, you need something," Mom pushed. "You don't have lunch till fifth period."

"Fine." I accepted the peach and sat down, taking a small bite and holding the peach in one hand while I scrolled through Instagram with my free one. Laura was doing a live video with the drama queens. They appeared to be doing their own version of Carpool Karaoke.

"Zoe? Zoe?" Mom sounded far away. "Zoe?" She put her hand over my phone screen, and I looked up. She wasn't smiling. "Be present, please."

"Mom!" It was my mother's favorite phrase these days: be present. Stop documenting every moment of your life, aka put away your phone. My parents didn't allow phones at the dinner table. There was a no-phones rule during family movie night, and no phones were allowed when we were in a restaurant. Even at home Mom was constantly complaining that Taryn, me, and even our dad were glued to our devices twenty-four seven. *When I'm sitting in front of you, I want to see your face, not you looking down at your phone,* she'd say.

"It's the first day of school," I reminded her. "I'm just looking to see who might be in my classes or on my bus." I looked up at her, unable to stop myself from making a dig. "Laura isn't taking it. She got a ride."

Last year Mom taught only part-time, so she drove me every day, but this year she had her own classroom and had to leave for school before my bus came. I was happy for her and all, but I was not thrilled about taking the bus. I had no clue who was even on my route. What if I had to sit alone every day? That would be the worst.

"I'm sorry," Mom said, and I felt bad. "Are you sure you don't want to get to school early and just go with me now?"

It was a nice offer, but the thought of standing outside Fairview alone while I waited for anyone I knew to show up sounded even worse than the bus. "No. It's okay, but thanks. You go and impress those second graders."

"Okay." Mom smiled and removed her hand from the

top of my phone and looked at me hopefully. "Have you spoken to Laura?"

Why did I say Laura's name? "I . . . Yes." It wasn't exactly a lie. I had texted her. Mom kept asking me what was going on with us, but I couldn't tell her Laura dropped me. She'd go running to Laura's mom again, and that would only make things worse.

"Oh good!" Mom played with her school ID, which was hanging from a lanyard around her neck. "Laura may not be on the bus, but Dianne said she has lunch fifth period, too, so at least you'll have someone to sit with." Mom hesitated. "She hasn't been over lately. Did something happen at the party?"

"We're fine."

"Okay. It's just that I know it was awkward seeing her there with other friends. But Dianne said—"

Time to change the subject. "Go! You can't be late," I reminded her.

"You're right!" Mom grabbed her bag and gave me a kiss on the cheek. "Make sure you lock up, and have a great day!"

"I will!" I lied.

I didn't have high hopes as I walked to the bus stop ten minutes later. It was only three houses down, so I could already see a group of boys waiting. Dougie Hoffman was one of them. He thought he was hilarious (he kind of was). There wasn't a single girl at the stop. I avoided eye contact, pulled out my phone, and scrolled through Instagram again. My posts were looking really sad and lonely. My last one was a picture of my plate with a giant red lobster and an ear of corn on it.

zonuts: Last lobster of the summer! Boo! #lobsters #Ilovesummer

Seriously, Zoe. That was the best you could come up with? A picture of a lobster?

It had gotten likes, though, even from Laura. She once told me she likes every photo in her feed, just so she gets likes back. Is that the only reason she liked mine?

The bus screeched to a halt, and the boys climbed on. I followed.

"Bus pass?" asked the driver. He was wearing a tee that said "Give Me a Brake." I guess he was trying to be funny, but he didn't look like he was in a joking mood.

In the corners of my mind, I remembered having a conversation with Mom about my bus pass last night, but I was also on the couch watching something on YouTube, so I might not have been paying her enough attention. I quickly checked my backpack pockets, hoping maybe she'd put it in one, but came up empty. My heart pounded. "I forgot it."

He sighed and waved me onto the bus. "Make sure you stop at the office and get a new one before you take the bus home."

"Thanks," I said, relieved. *Remember to get a bus pass! Don't tell Mom you forgot it!* I told myself as I headed down the aisle. The bus was packed, loud, and smelled like old socks. I held my breath and searched for an empty row.

"Zoe!"

I spotted Reagan and Jada waving to me and made a beeline for them. I'd never been so relieved to see them in my life. We hadn't spoken since Laura's birthday party. The whole situation was so awkward I didn't know what to say.

"You're alive! Where have you been?" Reagan asked as I slid in across from them. Her light blond hair was pulled back in a ponytail, and she was wearing a blue-and-orange Sharks tee, which was our school's mascot. Reagan played for the lacrosse team. The bus bumped along to the next stop. "We haven't seen you in weeks."

"We." That was a word best friends used to answer as a pair. Unlike Laura and I, summer hadn't ruined their BFF status. They even had identical teal backpacks for seventh grade.

"We Snapped you to go to the mall last week after my dance tryouts," Jada added. She was playing with a strand of her short black hair, which she kept curling and uncurling around her finger. "I made the upper-level team at my studio this year! Hey. Did you get braces?"

My hand went to my mouth subconsciously. "Yeah. Last week."

Jada nodded. "No wonder we didn't hear from you. When I got mine on, they hurt so much I couldn't eat for a week."

"I've been living on shakes," I said, happy to not have to reveal the real reason I went MIA. Honestly, I didn't want to see anyone after what happened with Laura. "That's great about dance. Sorry I didn't text you guys back."

"It's okay," Jada said. "We were shopping for back-to-school outfits and wanted you to come. Be honest." She held up her backpack. Her brown eyes were full of worry. "Is this babyish? Or cute? Because now I'm second-guessing the teal."

"I like the teal!" Reagan said. "Zoe, tell her teal is a great color."

"I like teal," I agreed, and Reagan smiled.

I noticed she was wearing black eyeliner, which made her dark eyes look even darker. Should I have worn eyeliner too? Was everyone wearing makeup to school in seventh grade? Mom still wouldn't let me wear more than mascara and lip gloss, even though Laura was allowed. (I assumed. She always had a full face of makeup on in posts.) I was relieved to see Jada didn't have any eyeliner on.

"Okay, I was just worried." Jada frowned. "Laura did a whole Insta story this weekend about middle school dos and don'ts, and her friend Ava said never carry a backpack unless it's black or brown and don't join nerdy clubs. Laura is definitely quitting Future City."

"Let her quit. Future City is not nerdy," Reagan snapped,

then looked at the two of us nervously. "Okay, maybe some people might think it's nerdy. . . ."

"But who cares? We're still allowed to like it," Jada said, as if trying to convince herself. "Just like I like this backpack."

I held up my old gray book bag. "I didn't even go shopping for a bag yet. My mom said Taryn bought three in seventh grade because she kept changing her mind on what would work best, so she wanted me to wait. Oh, and I'm sticking with Future City this year too."

Reagan beamed. "Did you see Ms. Pepper's post on the club board last night?"

"Yes! I think this means we're going to be creating a clean water program for urban development," Jada said excitedly. "And the regional competition, if we make it, is in Washington, DC!"

"I started working on a clean water filter this morning." It felt good to share the news with someone. Normally I would have told Laura first.

"Cool!" Jada said. "I did one of those this summer for fun, and . . ."

I tuned out, thinking again about Laura. Would she really quit Future City? What if she was right about it being nerdy? Did I really need to start worrying about what people thought of the club I was in? My cheeks flushed.

"Are you going to volleyball tryouts today?" Reagan asked, and I was pulled from my worries again.

"Uhhh . . . yes," I said, even though my stomach immediately tightened at the thought. I'd been trying to forget about tryouts. They were all Taryn talked about with me. *You'd better make the team. I did! I was pulled up to high school level in eighth grade!* But what if I didn't make it? I loved playing, but there were only so many slots on the middle school team. With everything going on with Laura, I'd even forgotten we had tryouts that afternoon. *Volleyball tryouts! Today! Remember!* I tried to remind myself. Maybe I should write these things down.

Reagan bit her lip. "I hope we all make it. I really want to play."

"You'll make it. You make every team," Jada said. "I'm the one who should be worried. I'm short, and that's a problem in volleyball."

"But you've got a great serve!" Reagan argued. "I'm the one that messes up whenever I'm the middle hitter. I get nervous."

"We're all going to do fine." Jada popped a mint into her mouth, then offered us both the container. I took one and let the minty flavor hit my tongue. "What period do you have lunch?"

"Fifth." That much I knew off the top of my head. Laura and the drama queens had posted their schedules, and they also had lunch fifth period. I thought again about what Mom said this morning. Should I try to sit with Laura and her friends?

34

"Us too!" Reagan said, sounding seriously happy, which made me happy, but also worried because what if there weren't enough seats for all of us to sit with Laura? Or what if Laura didn't invite us over? My first day was feeling complicated already, and we hadn't even arrived at school yet.

"What period do you have Spanish?" Jada asked.

I reached in my bag for my schedule . . . then remembered I'd folded it up and tucked it into my green glitter phone wallet—the wallet I ripped off the case last night because it was identical to the one Laura used. Or used to use. She'd posted a mirror selfie over the weekend, and I noticed right away Laura had gotten a new phone case, and a red sticky wallet with an *Annie* logo on it. She was slowly replacing our friendship piece by piece. I was so upset I ripped my wallet off too . . . and now I could clearly see in my mind the schedule still tucked inside and lying on my desk. "I left my schedule at home." My heart started to pound. "What do I do?"

"I think they can print it for you in the main office," Jada said. "I wrote mine supersmall so I could hide it in my notebook. See?" She held up an index card with writing so tiny it could be read only by mice. "That way no one will know I don't have it memorized yet."

"Where is the main office, again?" Reagan asked as the bus stopped at the next stop and three more kids climbed on. It was so loud, I could barely hear Reagan anymore.

"First floor. I think?" Jada sounded unsure, though. "I

never went there last year, but it has to be by the principal's office."

"The principal's office?" I was going to hyperventilate. "I don't want to go anywhere near there." No one wanted to be on Principal Higgins's radar. She called everyone sweetie, but she was really strict. She was also constantly giving people detention for any minor infraction you could think of.

"You're going to be fine! Do you remember any of your classes?" Reagan asked. "What do you have first period?"

"Math. I *think*." I racked my brain. "Or is it social studies? I remember something about a room 132."

Reagan perked up. "That's good! If you know the room number, that has to be where you're supposed to be first period, because you'd memorize first period first. Right?" I nodded. "What else do you remember?"

I bit my lip. "Nada."

"Find the main office," Jada said as she tried to apply lip gloss using her camera. The bus hit a bump, and she wound up drawing on her nose. "You have ten minutes before the first bell. You'll be fine."

I had only ten minutes? Why couldn't this bus go faster?

"Maybe we'll have a class together," Reagan said as a wad of paper flew by her head. There was a sudden stop and then yelling by the bus driver. "If not, at least we're in lunch, right?"

"Do you have any classes with Laura?" Jada asked. "If you do, you could text her and ask where to go."

I looked away and saw a boy stick gum under his seat. Gross. "I haven't spoken to her in a while." *Since the birthday party that wasn't.*

"We haven't either," Jada admitted, and I looked at her.

"Not since the party," Reagan added.

As best friends, they usually finished each other's sentences.

Laura and I used to do that.

Jada made a face. "She's been so . . ."

But she didn't get to finish the thought. The bus ground to a halt in front of the school, and people immediately started filing off. I looked out the window and saw a sea of teachers and crossing guards directing kids past the main doors. Everyone except me looked like they knew where to go. Jada and Reagan followed me off the bus, and I tried to remember to breathe. *Go to the main office. The main office!*

"Oh, Zoe, I think you have something on your jeans." Jada poked me in the butt. "Sorry! Is that mud?"

"Where?" I tried to swivel to look, but my head didn't rotate that far. "Nooo! It must be from my experiment this morning."

"It's small," Reagan said. "I'd rub it, but then I'd be touching your butt, and that would look weird. Just run to the bathroom and wash it off."

"She doesn't have time!" Jada told her. "She has to go to the main office and get her schedule *and* make it to first period, all in the next ten minutes." Jada smiled. "You can't *really* see it. Just pull your shirt down."

I tugged on my tee, stretching it out. I hoped it covered the spot. Why had I worn white?

There was the roar of an engine, and the three of us looked at the street. A motorcycle pulled up to the curb with two riders. A girl in a purple helmet climbed off the back.

"Is that Clare?" Reagan asked.

"It looks like it," Jada said.

I watched Clare swing her leg over the side of the bike and climb off. She removed her helmet and shook out her short brown hair, which was shaved short on one side. The tips of her hair were bright pink. You had to admire a girl who could rock a purple Batgirl tee and cheetah-print leggings on the first day of school. The first bell rang, and she gave us a wave, not even stopping to say hi.

"We should get to our lockers," Reagan said, sounding nervous. "My lock keeps getting stuck, so part of me thinks I should just carry my books all day. What if I can't open the locker later?"

We were all starting to panic. I couldn't go to my locker even if I wanted to because the number was written on my schedule! Mom had offered to take me to see my locker last week, but I hadn't wanted to run into Laura, so we didn't go. I was already regretting that decision.

"Everything is going to be fine," Jada said, but as we entered school, her right eye was twitching. "My first class is upstairs. I'll see you at lunch, Zoe."

"Mine too," said Reagan, consulting her schedule. "See you later." She disappeared into the crowd.

"See you!" I said, trying to remain upbeat. I knew I'd been out of school for a few months, but the main office couldn't be that hard to find. Finally spotting the sign for the office down the hall, I squeezed through a group of girls talking about their summer vacations and darted inside. There was a line of kids already.

"If you need to print your schedule, it's going to be a while," said a woman behind the counter as if she were reading my mind. "The printer is out of ink, and we're waiting for someone to bring more." There was a collective groan. "We'll take you one by one, and you can write it down instead."

Someone tapped me on the shoulder. It was Clare. "Hey."

"Hey!" I said, feeling relieved. "You lost your schedule too?"

"No." Clare shook her head. "I wanted to tell you there's something on your jeans."

My stomach did a back flip. I guess my shirt wasn't covering the stain. "Is it that bad?"

Clare cocked her head to one side. "Kind of? But don't panic. I could walk behind you to first period if you want. We both have math."

That was so nice of her. Wait. "We have class together? How do you know that?"

Clare looked at me strangely. "You posted your schedule to your Instagram story. I think we have the same schedule all morning, except for sixth period."

I completely forgot I did that! That meant I had a picture of my schedule on my phone! I fished it out of my bag and fired up Instagram. Just as the app sprang to life, someone yanked the phone out of my hand. "Hey—oh. Good morning, Principal Higgins." I stared with trepidation at the short, heavyset woman in a blue dress.

"Sweetie, there is no social media use in school," my principal reminded me. "There is no phone use at all unless specified by class, as you should know if you consulted your student handbook. I'm going to need to hold on to this for the day."

"But you don't understand. I forgot my schedule at home, and the printer here is out of ink. I have it on my phone. I just want to write it down." She continued to stare at me, and I felt my face grow hot. Everyone on line was looking at me. "That's the only reason I had it out."

Principal Higgins nodded. "That may be, but rules are rules." Her tone was friendly, but I got the impression she was not going to negotiate. "You can have it back after school." I watched her place my phone in a basket with other phones. It looked sad, probably like I did now. "The secretary will print you your schedule."

"But she just said the printer is out of ink," Clare tried, but Principal Higgins was already confiscating the next phone she saw.

"Now what?" I moaned. "If you pull out your phone, she'll take yours too."

"I know." Clare made a face. "But don't worry. "Don't worry," she assured me when she saw my reaction. "I've got our schedule memorized. Let's ditch this line and stop at the bathroom first so you can clean that spot on your pants." Clare opened the door. "You coming?"

I hesitated. The heat of the hallway and the sound of a thousand students filled the air.

To me, it was the sound of doom.

CHAPTER FOUR

There was no time for the bathroom. By the time we got out of the main office, we had less than three minutes to get from one end of the school to the other for first-period announcements. And second-period science was back near the main office, but on the second floor. I wonder if they'd consider letting me drop gym. I was getting enough of a workout running from class to class.

Science, though, was a pick-me-up. Our teacher said we were going to learn about fossils, coral reefs, and the human heart this year, all of which I couldn't wait to study. But after that period, I was back to being stressed again.

Clare stood behind me as we walked to each class, which was nice, but also made it look like I was walking alone, and she had to keep yelling out directions over the music they pumped in the hallways between periods. I didn't see

Laura, Reagan, or Jada anywhere. People moved so fast, it was hard to see anyone. It felt like all my classes were filled with kids from other elementary schools instead of my old one, so I didn't recognize anyone. By fourth-period Spanish, I had completely stretched out my shirt trying to hide the stain on my jeans.

"Cómo te llama?" the teacher greeted me as I walked into the classroom.

I froze. Laura and Sarah were seated side by side in the front row. Laura and I made eye contact. She smiled. For a split second, I felt hopeful again, but then she turned back to Sarah as if I were just a random student.

"Me llamo es Clare Stelton." Clare sounded fluent. The teacher looked at me next.

"Uh . . . see llamas Zoe Mitchell." Clearly I hadn't practiced over the summer.

The teacher checked her clipboard and shook her head. "You're in my sixth-period class, not fourth."

Wait, what? If I wasn't supposed to be in Spanish, what class was I supposed to be in? We'd had math, science, and English already. What else was there? Clare mouthed, "Sorry." Laura and Sarah looked at me curiously. I exhaled slowly. I was not going to get upset, even if the entire class was staring at me. "Sorry. I lost my schedule," I lied.

The teacher gave me a look and went to her desk. "I'll call down to the main office to find out where you should be. Hang on."

The rest of the class took the two-second break as an excuse to start talking. Clare took a seat. I stood by awkwardly, staring at the clock on the wall as if it were the most fascinating clock in the world.

"Zoe!"

I heard my name and looked up. Laura was waving me over. I glanced quickly at the teacher on the phone, then rushed over to Laura's desk. Laura wanted to talk to me! Maybe she was going to ask me to sit with them at lunch. "Hey," I said, trying not to sound too excited.

"I just wanted to tell you you've got a stain on the back of your jeans," Laura whispered.

I prayed my face wasn't turning purple. That's why she'd called me over? "Oh. Yeah," I said quickly. "I know."

"You know?" Laura's eyes bulged out. There was nothing she hated more than a ruined outfit.

"Zoe Mitchell?" the teacher called out to me. "You're supposed to be in health in room 205. Since you're late, stop down at the main office to get a late pass first."

This had to be some sort of joke. Why couldn't she just give me a late pass? "Thanks," I said, backing out of the room so that my black hole of a stain wasn't seen by everyone.

"You've got something on your jeans," said an eighth grader as I backed out of the classroom.

I was growing more mortified by the second.

The main office was at the other end of the building,

of course. By the time I got through another long line of lost students waiting for schedule changes or answers to questions like *What do I do if my locker won't open?*, health was almost over.

"Here," a weary secretary said when I finally made it to the front. (The printer had ink again. Yay.) "And here's a late pass for— Oh." The bell rang. "Fourth period is over. You have lunch fifth. No pass needed, but I'd get going if I were you. The line to buy gets long."

Long was right. By the time I made it to Cafeteria A, the line to buy was wrapped around the room. I joined the queue and scanned the crowd for anyone I knew. Sixth graders had their own cafeteria, but in seventh and eighth grades, students were mixed together, and the room was jammed and very loud. I was thankful the noise drowned out my stomach growling as we inched closer to the head of the long line. Why had I thought it was a good idea to buy on the first day? It took twenty minutes to get to the front.

"You've got five minutes till the end of the period," said one of the lunch aides as she dumped a very burnt-looking hamburger onto my plate. "You better eat fast."

I quickly paid and went back into the cafeteria to find somewhere to sit, but I was too late. On my left Laura was sitting with Sarah and the other drama queens, and there wasn't a seat to spare at their table. I shifted the weight of my tray and turned to my right to look around for Jada and

Reagan, but I didn't see them. All I saw was Jake Graser's crew tossing chips into one another's mouths. I couldn't keep standing there looking lame. What was I going to do? I looked at Laura again and hesitated. Should I walk over and attempt to talk to her again? *Look up, Laura. Look up so I can ask you!*

"Dougie, catch!" a guy shouted.

I turned around in time to see an apple fly past my head. My body flew forward as someone bumped into me from behind, sending my tray flying. It landed with a spectacularly loud crash. The cafeteria went completely silent.

"Score!" yelled a boy from the back of the room, and a group of guys cheered. I felt my face burn. *Don't cry. Don't cry. Don't cry.*

Dougie slid to the ground and grabbed my burger, which was now bunless. My fries had spilled all over the floor. "You okay? I'm sorry about that."

"Don't worry about it," I said, not making eye contact as I quickly grabbed my dropped water bottle and chips and placed them back onto the tray. I hurried to the garbage can and dumped the tray to destroy the evidence. I did not want to think about all the eyes on me. Laura had always been the first one to come to my aid if I screwed up, or at the very least say something silly to make me laugh. She'd always say, *Do you know how many views you would have had if we recorded that? We'd be millionaires!* Despite my better judgment, I felt myself search for her now. I was surprised to find her looking right at me. For just a moment, I thought she was going to get up and help me. Instead, she gave me the smallest of sad smiles and went back to her conversation.

My best friend was officially gone.

The bell rang, and my humiliation was quickly forgotten as people streamed past me to get to their next class. I joined the crowds again and made it to my next class—technology—on time, but died a little when I realized the class was with Laura and Sarah again.

"Pick a partner," the tech teacher said. "You'll have the same one all quarter."

"Sarah!" Laura said before the teacher even finished the sentence. The two of them hugged. I felt like I was having an out-of-body experience.

"You want to work together?" asked a girl I didn't know.

"Sure," I said, but inside, it felt like another blow. I just wanted this day to be over already. After eighth-period social studies, I practically ran to the main office to get my phone back. There was no line this time. In fact, the place was deserted. "Hello?"

Someone popped up from behind the counter. "Hi there! How can I help you?"

The cranky woman from this morning had been replaced by a smiling redhead wearing purple glasses and thick gold pearls. Her cropped blue sweater and skirt screamed 1950s costume party. I knew that only because we'd had a 1950s party in sixth grade. Laura and I had decided to wear matching poodle skirts. At the last minute Laura showed up in hot pink satin pants like some of the other drama queens had. I should have known then that things were headed south.

"Principal Higgins took my phone this morning and said I could have it back after school. My name is Zoe Mitchell. My phone has a gold case with glitter."

"Cute! Okay. She took a lot of phones. Hang on while I find the basket." She practically skipped away from the counter, humming a tune I didn't recognize, and headed into another room.

I wasn't anywhere near that upbeat. I just wanted to go home. As soon as the woman turned away, I leaned my elbows on the counter and placed my head in my hands, trying hard not to cry. "Hang in there a half hour more, Zoe," I told myself. "Do not cry. Who am I kidding?" I laughed as tears started to stream down my cheeks. "You already are crying! And why shouldn't you? This was the worst first day ever." I wiped my eyes. "I wish I could just go back and do it all over."

"Your first day was that bad, huh?"

I looked up, startled. How much had this woman heard? Wasn't she just in the other room? I noticed her eyes were almost yellow in the bad fluorescent light. She was frowning ever so slightly.

"Be honest: Was it that bad?"

"Yes," I admitted. It felt good to say it out loud. "And now I just want to go home." She nodded sympathetically.

Who cared about volleyball tryouts? There was no way I'd perform well after the day I'd had. I'd probably set the ball and accidentally break someone's nose. As soon as I got my phone, I'd be out of there. But that meant I needed my bus pass because I wouldn't be getting a ride. "Can you print me a bus pass while I'm here too?" I asked.

"Umm . . . I'm not sure. I'm just a temp!" The woman laughed. "Anyway, here are the phones." She placed a basket on the counter, and we fished through it. There had to be a dozen phones in there. "Huh. That's funny," she said. "There's no phone with a sparkly case."

"It has to be here," I said, looking through the basket a second time. But she was right. My phone was MIA. That's when I started to panic. "I saw Principal Higgins put it in here! Is there another place she keeps people's phones?" I looked around the empty office, half-hoping to see a tower of confiscated phones somewhere, but there was none.

"No need to panic!" the woman yelled from under the table she was currently checking. "Let me just radio Principal Higgins." I heard a walkie-talkie in her hand crackle to life. "Ms. Higgins? Marge Simpkins temping in the main office. A phone has gone rogue. Do you copy?" All I heard was static from the other end. "Huh. She's probably on bus duty!" She popped back up from under the table and smiled brightly. "They're getting ready to leave."

I glanced at the clock on the wall. I now had exactly two minutes to make it to Bus Eight. I groaned. "I know. I'm supposed to be on one."

"Oh boy!" she chuckled. "Let me look faster! Maybe there are more phones hidden in the assistant principal's office. Hang tight." She ran off again.

I heard her moving around the room as the clock ticked down to the bus's departure. Going, going, gone. Great. Now what?

"Found it!" She rushed out of the office holding a phone with a glittered case. "I knew it was somewhere! You're all set for tomorrow, if you're still here."

"Still here?" I repeated. Of course I'd be here. It was the second day of school. I still had 178 to suffer through. "I don't really think I have a choice."

She patted my arm and smiled. "Don't you worry, sweetie. I have a feeling it will be a whole new world when you wake up tomorrow morning. You'll see!"

She was still smiling at me as I exited the office. How could someone be that perky and work in a middle school? And how did she know day two would be better than day one? Today had been a disaster, and now I had to walk home in ninety-degree weather. The bus was gone, Mom and Dad were still at work, and Grandma was on a cruise to Bermuda, so there was zero chance of getting a ride. I went to text Mom and realized my phone was off. Ms. Higgins must have done that. I pressed power, and my phone sprang to life with text messages.

> **Jada:** Were you at lunch? R and I didn't see you! U OK?
> **Reagan:** Where are you??? Tryouts are starting!
> **Unknown:** Sry. Thought we had the same sched.
> **Unknown:** This is Clare btw.

I felt bad when I read their texts, but I had no energy to respond. Besides, I was allowed to change my mind about joining the volleyball team, wasn't I? Laura had. Maybe I could convince my parents to homeschool me. They were teachers. Couldn't they make that happen?

My phone locked, returning to the lock screen's photo of Laura and me. It was one we took on the sixth-grade boat trip around Manhattan. We had our arms wrapped around each other on the dance floor. I loved this picture, but it didn't tell the whole story. We actually spent most of the boat ride apart. She had hung out inside at a table with the drama queens, and I had sat outside with Reagan and Jada on the outdoor deck, taking in the view. I think I knew something was changing, even back then. But then suddenly our favorite Ariana Grande song came on, and Laura appeared, grabbed my hand, and swung me onto the dance floor. We sang and danced our hearts out for three minutes, and at the end, she pulled me into this selfie. She posted it with the hashtag #bestiesforlife.

How had we gone from best friends to total strangers in just a couple of months? Laura had completely ghosted me. She'd dropped me to hang with Sarah and the drama queens so she could have the #bestpizzaever every day of the week. My finger hovered over the Instagram app to check on what she was up to.

Don't look at Laura's posts, Zoe, a voice inside my head pleaded, but I ignored it.

Laura had posted a picture eight minutes earlier. She and the drama queens weren't having pizza. They were in someone's pool, and she and Sarah were sitting on people's shoulders and wearing similar black bikinis. Bikinis! Laura always said she hated showing her stomach, and now she was wearing a bikini? The photo had several hashtags: #BestFirstDay #Nohomework #SummerIsntOverYet.

They'd just gotten home. How were they already in the pool and posting photos?

Don't look at her old posts again! the voice screamed at me.

I ignored it.

I'd examined her last two weeks of summer posts a thousand times. Laura at the mall with Sarah, meeting a YouTuber! Laura zip-lining at an adventure park with the drama queens! Laura and Sarah learning how to surf (*surf?*)! Laura and the drama queens at sunset on the beach! Their posts were perfectly angled and filtered. They each had more than two hundred likes, and dozens of comments. Even their outfits were coordinated—how else could you explain how every one of them always seemed to have something pink on, or the same blue scrunchie? I didn't see in any of her pictures the sneakers Laura and I spent weeks glittering or any of the shirts we'd gotten at boutique shops at the shore that said things like "Sea la Vie." She certainly wasn't wearing her Future City club tee like I had all summer. Even Laura's hair looked different, like she'd had it professionally highlighted. Mom still wouldn't let me use that sort of dye on my head.

When I looked back at my feed and our pictures, the posts were snoozefests and infrequent. Before the boat picture our last one together had been taken in my tree house, and we had been playing Jenga. The one before that was taken in front of our Future City development model. Our shots seemed babyish, while her new posts (two or three a day) screamed middle school cool.

Laura had upgraded friends. It was that simple.

A big fat tear fell onto my phone, and then another. I quickly rubbed them away with my finger, wishing I could erase the last few months.

"Zoe?"

I looked up. Clare was standing in front of me.

"Do you need a ride?" she asked. "I missed the bus too."

I wiped my eyes again. "Oh. I . . . I'm not sure my mom would want me on a motorcycle, but thanks."

Clare laughed. "We have a car too." She pointed to the SUV at the curb. "I am never allowed on her bike either, other than the first day of school. It's tradition."

"Oh!" What a fun tradition. "Sure. That would be great."

Clare nodded to the car. "Come on, then. Let's get out of here already."

I followed Clare to the car. I couldn't agree more.

CHAPTER FIVE

Clare's mom tried to ask us about our first day, but neither of us was chatty. Clare seemed as fried as I did, which made me wonder what her day had been like. I didn't press her in front of her mom. Instead I just enjoyed the air-conditioned silence. It was ninety degrees and our school's air-conditioning was mediocre at best. By the time Clare's mom dropped me off, I was parched. When I got home, I went straight past Taryn in the kitchen and grabbed a drink from the fridge. I immediately started to gag. The chocolate milk must have turned. I spit it out in the sink.

"Ewwwwwwww! Zoeeeeeeeee! Gross! I'm FaceTiming!" Taryn complained as I continued to hack. "What's wrong with you?" She and Avery, whose tiny face appeared in Taryn's phone screen, waited for a response.

Did Taryn actually want me to answer? Or did she just

want me to disappear so she could get back to talking to Avery? I didn't care if she wanted to talk or not. I needed to tell *someone* what had happened, and Laura wasn't that person anymore. "I forgot my bus pass and my schedule, and when I went to look it up on my Insta, where I posted it, Principal Higgins saw me and took my phone away," I blurted out. "But the main office couldn't print my schedule either because its printer ran out of ink, so I had to rely on Clare, who got my schedule wrong, so I showed up in the wrong class, was late to others, and then dropped my tray in front of everyone and on top of everything I spent the whole day walking around with a stain on my white pants that looked like poop! *That's* what's wrong."

Taryn and Avery both looked at me and started laughing.

"Zoe, you're too funny," Avery said. "No one's first day is *that* awful!"

"Yeah! You're exaggerating!" Taryn said. "Aren't you?" They both looked at me expectantly.

I instantly regretted opening my mouth. "Yep. Like Mom would say, I was just being dramatic."

"I knew it." Taryn rolled her eyes and turned back to Avery. "So what were you saying before Zoe came in and yakked?"

"Oh! I said I am so glad we start volleyball tomorrow," Avery said. "I'm so bored, aren't you?"

"Yes," Taryn agreed, winding a lock of hair around her finger. "Who wants to sit home alone when you could be practicing with the team?"

I hadn't thought of that when I made the rash decision to skip tryouts. What would I do all afternoon if I had no sport and I couldn't be in Future City because everyone thought it was nerdy? Lying on the couch was fun for a day or two. Not a whole year. Plus, there was the fact that Mom would kill me if I was home all the time.

"Hellooooo, Zooooeeee!"

Taryn was staring at me again. "Avery asked when your tryouts are."

I felt my stomach tighten. How could I skip the first day of tryouts? There was no way I'd make the team now. "They haven't announced them yet," I lied.

Avery whistled. "Here we go. . . ."

"Avery?" Taryn said sweetly. "I'll call you back." Taryn hung up and pointed a purple-painted fingernail at me. "Liar! High school had their tryouts last week, but middle school always has them the first week of school. Meaning today. And you missed them! Coach Carr texted me!"

My eyes nearly bulged out of my head. "Why'd you ask if you already knew?"

"This is so like you! Why didn't you go? You *like* volleyball. I put myself out there and told Coach Carr how good you are!"

"You did?" I was surprised Taryn had gone to bat for

me, but maybe she had an ulterior motive. "I mean, why are you butting in? Who texts with their middle school volleyball coach?"

Taryn crossed her arms. "Why didn't you go today? This better not be about Laura."

Was I supposed to tell Taryn the truth? That I couldn't imagine surviving another two hours of school? That between Laura's early-morning bagel run without me, not inviting me to sit with her at lunch, and picking another partner in technology class, I felt like I was dying inside even though I wasn't supposed to let her get to me? Or would she just laugh at me again? Instead, I said nothing.

Taryn stared me down. "I swear, if you ruin the Mitchell reputation, I will never forgive you." She sighed and started texting. "I'm telling Coach Carr you got food poisoning and went home after school, but you'll be at the second tryout tomorrow. I'm saying not to hold this against you because you will wow her with your skills. Get out your phone and put in a reminder."

I resisted the urge to bear-hug her (Taryn hasn't hugged me in years). "Thank you, thank you, thank—"

"Don't thank me yet—you still have to make the team! I told her you're not as good as I am, but she needs you." Taryn poked me in the shoulder. "So don't mess this up." Her face softened. "Besides, the team will give you a chance to meet new people." My phone pinged, and Taryn looked at it. "Is that Miss Hashtag Best First Day Ever?"

"You mean Laura?" I asked.

"Yes, Laura! That pool picture she posted was so staged—it wasn't even taken today. They all had on the same bathing suits that they did yesterday!"

"They did?" I hadn't noticed that.

"Yes. Girls like her take a slew of pictures so they have posts for days." Taryn stared at my phone. "Seriously, unfollow her."

"You're following her," I pointed out.

"Not anymore!" Taryn swiped to her Instagram right in front of me, went to Laura's profile, and hit unfollow. My jaw fell. Laura checked her followers. She would notice Taryn was gone. "Now you do it!"

But I couldn't cut the cord. Laura was my best friend. Or had been. Even if she was ready to drop me from her life, I wasn't ready to cut her out of mine. Following her Insta might be the only way I'd know what she was up to. I clutched my phone. "No."

Taryn tried to pry the phone from my hand. "Do it!"

The two of us struggled for a moment before the phone slipped from my hands and went flying across the floor. I rushed over to grab it.

"It's not cracked, is it?" Even she looked concerned.

Our parents were always threatening us about taking good care of our phones because they were a privilege, not a right, and all that stuff about responsibility. I'd only gotten a phone the spring of sixth grade, while Laura had gotten one from her dad at the end of fifth, when her parents got divorced. I was desperate not to break mine. Once, Taryn cracked her phone screen, and Dad made her save up enough babysitting money to fix it before she could take it to the store to be replaced.

Sometimes I wondered if Mom held off getting me a phone even longer because Dianne complained Laura never put her phone down. *She's obsessed with it,* Dianne would say, and then the two would compare apps that were appropriate for our age. Laura was always able to download all of them before I could. Thankfully, Mom let me have an Instagram account as long as I set it to private.

Please don't be broken. Please don't be broken. I took a deep breath and picked up my phone. Not broken! Not even a crack on it. But what was this new app open on the screen? "It's fine," I told my sister. "No thanks to you."

Taryn sighed. "Good. Now go away. Just be at tryouts tomorrow." Taryn grabbed a bag of pretzels from behind me and FaceTimed Avery again.

I stared at my phone. The app had no name, just a pink-and-gold icon. That was strange. I hadn't downloaded this app. Was this definitely my phone? Maybe that crazy office employee gave me the wrong one. I looked from the glittered case to the home screen again. *Yes, it's your phone, silly. You're on the screensaver!*

"Hi, girls!" Mom walked in the front door balancing a stack of books in her arms. I rushed over to help her.

"Thanks, Zo-Zo. How was your first day of seventh grade? Who was in your classes? Did you meet anyone new? Do you like your teachers? How was Spanish class? How were volleyball tryouts? And the seventh-grade cafeteria?"

Mom had a habit of rapid-firing questions. The good news was she only remembered about half of what she asked you. "I sat with Reagan and Jada on the bus," I offered, skipping the volleyball discussion entirely.

Mom smirked. "So you *did* hear me last night and remembered to put the bus pass in your bag! I kept telling you it was still on your desk, but you were buried in your phone. Dad said to stop reminding you since you're in seventh grade now, but I hated the thought of you getting on the bus and realizing you didn't have it."

I could feel my cheeks warm. "Yeah, that would have been a bad start to the morning."

"Coach had a meeting today during lunch—I made JV captain in volleyball!" Taryn yelled from the kitchen.

"That's wonderful!" Mom said, walking into the room. I followed, panicked that the word "volleyball" was even being mentioned. *Please don't tell Mom, Taryn.*

Meanwhile, Taryn pursed her lips as she continued to Facetime Avery. "Zoe forgot her bus pass and skipped volleyball tryouts, and the principal took her phone."

"Taryn!" I yelled.

"It's true!" Taryn shouted.

Mom pointed to Taryn's phone. "Hang up with Avery,

please. And go upstairs. Now." Taryn stood up and stomped away. Mom turned to me. "You got your phone taken away? And you skipped tryouts? Zoe." She shook her head, disappointed. "What am I always saying about being present?"

"I forgot tryouts, okay? There was a lot going on today." My heart was beating fast. "And it didn't matter that I forgot my pass. Clare's mom gave me a ride home because I missed the bus."

Mom frowned. "Wait. Who is Clare?"

That was what Mom had taken away from this conversation?

"Clare. I invited her to the cabana for"—I didn't actually want to say "Laura's birthday"—"the party."

"Oh right! Why didn't you just call Dianne?" Mom asked. "She picked up Laura and a bunch of girls this afternoon. Why didn't you go with them? Did Laura invite you? You had classes together today, right?"

The Laura inquisition was starting. This was my cue to exit. "Um, I'm going to go upstairs and cover my books and stuff."

Mom studied me for a moment quietly, and I held my breath, wondering if there would be follow-up questions. Instead, she dismissed me. "Just be ready to leave in an hour." I walked past her and headed up the stairs. "We have Izumi reservations at five."

In the past we always had first-day-of-school dinner with Laura's family. But after what happened at the beach,

I assumed both of our moms agreed to cancel. Looking at my mom's smiling face, I could only assume one thing: She didn't realize how bad things had gotten between me and Laura. How did I get out of dinner without explaining what was going on?

Taryn rushed back downstairs. "Mom, nooooo. We cannot go out to dinner with Laura's family tonight!"

Mom blinked. "Why not?"

Taryn and I briefly glanced at each other and I knew for once we were on the same team.

"Because I'm too old to have dinner with the twins," Taryn said smoothly. "Who am I supposed to talk to?"

"You can survive one dinner. It's tradition," Mom said. "Dianne even got a reservation for the private room tonight."

Laura and I always liked the private room because it had glass walls and we had our own hibachi chef. Key word: "liked."

"Zoe just threw up," Taryn blurted.

I nodded. "It's true. I didn't want to tell you, but . . ."

"It was all over the kitchen," Taryn added. "I cleaned it up."

"Really well," I chimed in.

"Are you all right?" Mom felt my forehead. "It's probably from being in a hot school all day." She ran into the bathroom and came back with a thermometer, popping it into my mouth before I could protest. The thermometer beeped ten seconds later. "No temperature. I think you're just overheated. Why don't you go lie down for an hour before dinner?" She looked at my sister. "And you're going too. It's tradition." Her face softened. "Besides, this is the first year Dianne is going without Darren. We can't make her go alone."

I knew how much Laura missed having her dad around. He'd moved upstate after the divorce and she saw him only once a month, if she was lucky. She didn't like to talk about it much. Now I felt bad.

"Okay. I'm sure I'll be fine in an hour," I said, and Taryn gave me a look.

Mom's face brightened. "Great! I'll tell your dad to meet us at the restaurant. He had a meeting after school."

"Yay, tradition." Taryn pumped her fist in the air and stomped up the stairs and to her room. So did I.

"Oh, and Zo-Zo?" Mom called back to me. "You might want to change your pants. There's a stain on the back of them."

For a Tuesday night the restaurant was packed. I assumed it was because everyone was celebrating the first day of school like we were. Everywhere I looked, chefs were flinging shrimp to customers or creating onion volcanos that they lit on fire. Waitresses hurried past with brightly

64

colored bottles of Ramune sodas with the marble at the top that descended into the drink when you popped the cap on the lid. Laura and I were obsessed with them. "Were." Who knew what she was into now?

My heart was beating wildly as my parents snaked through the restaurant, following the hostess to the private room. In a panic, I pulled out my phone. YouTube. Instagram. Twitter. Maybe if I looked busy—maybe if I *was* busy—I wouldn't freak out about having to make small talk with my ex-BFF. Taryn and I walked behind my parents. I felt Taryn put her hand on my arm.

"Do you want my advice about this dinner, or do you only take advice from Laura?" she whispered.

I spun around, surprised. "Of course I want your advice; you just never give me any. What should I do?"

"Be friendly enough for Mom not to notice anything is wrong, but not so friendly that you look pathetic." She exhaled long and slow, and her voice dropped even lower. "This happened to me once too, and I know it's hard, but trust me, you do not want an ex-friend thinking you're obsessed with them."

I didn't know Taryn had friend problems. "What happened to you?"

"It doesn't matter. Just know I've got your— HEY!" Taryn noticed a group of girls waving to her. "What are you doing here?" She turned to me. "Are you going to be okay if I hang here for a few?"

The other girls looked at me, and my stomach tightened. Taryn was supposed to be my wingwoman in there. But what was I supposed to say? "I'll be fine."

I was officially on my own.

The hostess held open the door to the private dining table. Laura's twin sisters, Paige and Petra, were already popping open blue Ramune sodas and talking animatedly to the waitress. Mom and Dad made a beeline for Dianne. That left me and Laura, who was already seated and looking at her phone.

Here went nothing.

I walked over. "Hey, Laura."

Laura looked up and smiled. "Zo-Zo!" Then she stood up and *hugged me.* "How was your first day? Did you ever find your schedule after I saw you in my Spanish class?"

My cheeks burned at the memory. "Yep! The rest of my day went smooth." *Not really.*

"Oh good!" Laura smiled. "Sorry I couldn't help you, but I did not want to start talking and get in trouble on the first day, you know?" Her blue eyes blinked rapidly. "Today was crazy! Going from Spanish to English on the other side of the building in three minutes is insane! And Senorita Browning seems tough." She handed me a pair of chopsticks, and we both got to work ripping open the paper packaging, snapping the chopsticks apart, and filing the top rough edge of the wood, like we always did.

"I know!" Was Laura really opening up to me? "And

what's with Mr. Goran spitting all over the front row while he talks in social studies?"

Laura threw back her head and her long blond hair touched her waist. "Eww! I was in the splash zone for about two minutes before I moved my seat." We both laughed, and it felt good.

"Anything to drink?" asked the waitress.

"Two blue raspberry sodas." Laura looked at me for confirmation. "Right?"

"Right," I said, surprised she was speaking for the two of us again.

"Girls!" Dad walked over with his camera. He's the only person I know who still takes pictures with a real camera and not a phone. "Say 'We're in seventh grade!'"

Laura threw her arm around me. "We're in seventh grade!" she shouted.

Satisfied, Dad went to bother Paige and Petra. Laura started giggling.

"OMG, I love your dad. He never leaves home without that camera, even though he has an iPhone! Remember that time he tried to take our picture at the opening of Burgeritos?"

I started to laugh too. "I got mad at him and started yelling on line."

Laura imitated my dad's voice. "'It's the first time you've ever had a burger in a tortilla. How can I not photograph it?'"

"By *not* photographing it!" I said, which is exactly what

I said at the time. I watched Dad taking a picture of the twins. "If you only knew how many photos I had to take on battlefields this summer."

Laura winced. "I never asked you how that went. Was it torture?"

"Torture." But even three weeks in the car living on fast food wasn't as torturous as coming home and realizing my best friend had dropped me. "What about you? How was playing Molly in *Annie*? I saw that video you posted from the 'Hard Knock Life' scene. You were really good."

Laura sat up straighter and smiled. "Thanks! I hated that we only had three performances. We really wanted you to see it."

"We." Laura had a new "we." Was it Sarah, or did she just mean her and her mom? I tried to hold it together. "And how was Lake George with your dad? You didn't post any pictures."

Laura's smile faded. "Yeah, I . . ." She looked over at Dianne talking to my mother and lowered her voice. "I felt funny posting because Mom wasn't there, you know? I didn't want it to look like we were having fun with-out her. . . ." She trailed off and looked at her plate. "It was our first separate family vacation, and it was a little weird."

"I get it." Weird was something I could understand.

"We went on the Minnehaha sunset cruise, rode a Jet Ski, did the usual horse-and-carriage ride, hit the water park. Paige and Petra didn't seem to care, but I thought it was strange. I mean, if you want us to get used to only seeing you once a month and loving it, then plan something different, you know?"

Laura was confiding in me just like I wanted. We hadn't talked like this in months! What if I said the wrong thing? I tried to keep my answers short. "I'm sorry."

She shrugged, showing off her sunburned shoulders. "Whatever. I'm pushing Mom to take us to Florida for Christmas." The waitress placed the sodas in front of us, and Laura passed me one. We both unwrapped the cap, snapped the cap into the top of bottle, and heard the satisfying pop as the marble in the soda dropped into the main part. "At least you got to do something new on vacation." She turned to her side. "Mom?" Laura called over to Dianne across the table. "Tell them we want the flaming onion tower! It's our *thing*."

Our thing. What was happening?

Were Laura and I okay again?

It sure felt that way. For the next hour we talked so much we almost missed the flaming-onion-volcano. We both put our phones away. She didn't mention the drama queens. I didn't mention the birthday disaster. We talked about *The Office* reruns (we were both still obsessed) and this app Laura had discovered that filters a tan onto your skin, even when you're pale. (This explained why the drama queens always looked so flawless.) We were acting normal. Laura-and-Zoe normal. And it felt great. So great that I felt relaxed enough to ask Laura what activities she was doing that fall.

Laura scrunched up her nose. "Not volleyball. That's for sure."

The chef slid the steak and shrimp I'd ordered onto my plate, next to the mountain of fried rice I loved. Suddenly I wasn't hungry.

"I told Mom I am not doing sports this year." She took the chicken from her plate and put it onto mine, then took my shrimp without even asking. It was how we always did it.

"Yes, you are!" Dianne yelled from across the table. It's amazing what great hearing moms have. Dianne looked at my mom. "I told her I want her to do at least two sports this year, and . . ."

The two started talking again, and Laura looked at me. "She's delusional. I'm not doing volleyball or track. Maybe lacrosse."

I pointed a chopstick at her. "You hate lacrosse. You said it was scary."

Laura blinked. "Well, I was wrong. Sarah plays, and she's been teaching me this summer. I might try it in the spring. I love watching Jake Graser play." She grinned. "Maybe we'll both play, and then he and I can practice together. Killer bees, that would be amazing."

"Killer bees?" Now it was my turn to blink.

Laura pushed her hair behind her right ear, and I noticed she had a second piercing. The earrings were tiny anchors. "Oh, it's just this thing Sarah and I made up." She started to giggle. "We were outside the *Annie* rehearsals, and there was a bee, and Sarah said it was a killer bee. Then I said let's kill all the bees, and I swear the bee heard us and started chasing us, so now it's what we say when we are really into something. It means, like, amazing. Definite." She shrugged. "It's our thing."

They had a thing now? We were the ones who had things!

"What about Future City? Are you still doing that?" I asked as the chef began tossing shrimp. Taryn still wasn't even in the room yet.

"I love Future City!" Laura said extra loud, then leaned closer to me. "I told my mom I'm doing it, but I'm not." She looked horrified. "No one does Future City in seventh grade. At least, that's what Ava told me. She was in *Annie,* too, and her older sister said some of these clubs are a social death sentence. Besides, there are so many cooler clubs to choose from, like a cappella group." I must have made a face, because she quickly backpedaled. "But if Future City is still your thing, then you should do it. It's just not mine anymore."

I wasn't sure what to say. That morning, when Reagan, Jada, and I were talking about this year's Future City project, I was already thinking of what I would create in our

SimCity computer program model. But hearing Laura, I felt funny again. Was a STEM club lame? If I liked it, did that make me lame too?

"I'm too busy for clubs anyway," Laura yammered on. "My first love is theater. I'm trying out for the fall drama, then the spring musical and another local theater production, so my schedule will be packed. Did you know if you're into theater, you can even apply to Sayerville High's On Tour drama program and go there instead of Fairview High? Sarah and I are definitely applying." She got a far-off look in her eyes. "Killer bees, that would be incredible if we both got in."

Now Laura was thinking of going with Sarah to a different high school? And she hadn't even thought to tell me? Everything about our friendship had changed so fast, I couldn't keep up.

Laura's phone pinged. She read the text and laughed, then put the phone down again. "Mom? It's almost seven."

Her mom frowned. "We're not done eating yet." She looked at my mom apologetically. "Some of Laura's new friends are rehearsing tonight for the upcoming play."

Now Laura was leaving the dinner, which I hadn't even wanted to go to?

Laura was texting away again. "You know, you really should try out, Zo-Zo! You'd be good. Think of how great we always sing together."

"In the car maybe, but you know I hate doing anything

in front of a crowd. Don't you remember what happened at Future City regionals last spring? I botched my part of the presentation and couldn't remember anything. Even the memory of that hot convention center room in New Jersey still makes me nauseous."

Laura sighed and pulled her hand away and I wasn't sure if it was because I was talking about Future City again, or because of my fear of public speaking. "You just have to practice more and you'll be fine. You know, Sarah says—"

I finally snapped. "I don't care what one of the drama queens thinks." I instantly regretted my choice of words, but it was too late.

Laura put her phone into her bag. "Drama queens? Is that what you think we are? Nice."

"I just meant because you're all in drama," I said quickly, but Laura ignored me and stood up.

"Mom? I told Sarah we'd pick her up at seven. We have to go," Laura announced.

"Sarah! Sarah!" the twins shouted as Taryn finally walked in.

"I love her," said Petra.

"She's the new you, Zoe," Paige added, and Taryn winced.

Laura caught my eye, but I looked away as if I hadn't heard. I stood up as well. "I'm just going to run to the bathroom," I told my mom, then I smiled at Laura. "Good luck with rehearsal."

"Thanks," Laura said awkwardly. "And hey . . . next time we do this, we'll have to make sure we have time for green-tea ice cream. It's the best."

"The best," I repeated, but we just looked at each other sadly before turning away.

I wasn't sure there would be a next time with green-tea ice cream.

Our moment—if I could even call it that—was already gone.

CHAPTER SIX

Nice move, Zoe.

Laura and I were getting along like we used to, and what did I do? Called Sarah a drama queen.

Why did I do that? *Why?*

I knew I should apologize, but bringing it up on text felt stupid, and I couldn't approach her at her locker because the drama queens would be with her. We weren't hanging out, and who knew when Mom and Dianne were going to get us together again? It could be a month or longer, and by then, it would be too late to say anything. Paige was already calling Sarah the new Zoe. I couldn't let things between us get any worse. I had to fix our friendship *now*.

But how?

Lying on my bed after dinner, I pulled out my phone and took a selfie. It felt important to show I wasn't upset that Laura and I had fought. I let my hair spill all around me on the pillow, and snapped three-quarters of my smiling face. I hashtagged it #firstdayinthebooks and uploaded it to Instagram.

As soon as I did, I saw Laura's latest post. She and five girls were sitting on someone's porch and holding what looked like scripts. *Rehearsing!* Laura had written along with the hashtags #getitrightordontdoitatall #bestiesboundforbroadway #killerbees #dramaqueens.

Was the "drama queens" hashtag a dig at me? I pictured Laura telling Sarah about what I said at dinner. *You know who's the real drama queen? Zoe. She can't accept that our friendship has been over for months.*

Tonight could have been my chance to smooth things over with Laura, and I'd blown it. What if I never got another chance to make things right? A tear fell onto my phone. I quickly rubbed it away, accidentally closing Instagram along with it. The icon for the new app stared back at me. It had a symbol of a camera with counterclockwise arrows surrounding it. Curious, I clicked on it.

Strangely, the app features were just like Instagram, with lots of people's photos and posts in a continuous scroll. I didn't recognize anyone I knew, so I kept scrolling till I landed on a picture that was familiar.

It was mine.

I sat up on my bed. How did this app have my Instagram pictures? Or a whole profile on me that I hadn't created?

I started clicking through my pictures and found one of Laura and me on a sleepover last spring. We were side by side in matching purple sleeping bags.

Laura's mom always let her do something over-the-top the weekend before school ended, and she always invited me to come along. One year we did Sephora makeovers, and another, facials. The sleepover had always been just the two of us, but this spring, Laura invited the drama queens to come, too, because they'd just started hanging out during the sixth-grade play. The drama queens wanted to spend the night pranking boys and playing this game called Truth or Text, which went really badly. Laura blamed me for what happened.

Looking at the picture of us again I wondered: If I had spent the sleepover talking to Laura about Jake's hair and his lacrosse team like Sarah and the drama queens did, would that have changed everything between us? Compared to Laura and her new friends, were my interests immature?

There was a knock on my door. "Zo-Zo? You still up?"

It was Mom. I quickly wiped my eyes. "Yeah. Just getting ready for bed."

Mom came in carrying a stack of laundry for me to put away. It smelled like baby powder, lavender, and fresh sheets rolled into one, kind of how my mom smelled. She took one look at me and just knew. "Hey. What's wrong?"

I didn't answer. I just started to cry harder.

Mom sat down on the edge of my bed and didn't say a word. Instead, she leaned in for a hug, and I crumbled into her.

"You're getting so big that I'll take these free hugs whenever I can get them," she said. "They're rare these days."

"I hugged you just last week," I told her shoulder.

"Yeah, because I gave you twenty dollars to get a new phone case."

"That was hugworthy!" I pointed out, and we both broke apart laughing.

"Was dinner okay tonight?" Mom asked suddenly. "I know Laura had to leave early. . . ."

My smile slipped at the mention of Laura. "It was fine."

"I didn't know Laura had other plans. Dianne said she's very into acting lately. If I had known she would leave before dessert, I would have—"

I just wanted to stop talking about Laura. "It's okay, Mom."

Mom pushed my hair off my face and stared back at me. "You know, seventh grade is a great time to meet some new people, try some new things."

"Mom." I turned away, realizing I sounded a lot like Taryn.

"I'm just saying, Laura is doing the school play instead of volleyball. Maybe it's time you branched out, too, and did something without Laura."

I blinked in surprise. "I like doing things with Laura."

"I know." Mom pulled at a loose thread on my quilt and yanked it out. "I just don't want to see you waiting around for her to call or text you when she's doing other things. If you really like volleyball and Future City, which I think you do, stick with them because *you* like them. Don't quit because Laura isn't doing them too."

"I'm not." But the word "immature" kept flashing through my mind.

"Good!" She patted my leg. "Maybe a break from Laura is a good thing."

"But I don't want a break from Laura," I said, a little taken aback Mom even suggested it. "She's my best friend."

"I know, but . . ." She hesitated. "What about those girls you like from Future City? Reagan and Jada? You invited them to Laura's birthday party. Where do they hang out? What do they do?"

Here came the questions. "I don't know. They're best friends. Like Laura and I." *Were,* I don't add. "They have each other. They don't need a third wheel."

"Not everyone only hangs out with one person," Mom reminded me. "Maybe those girls are hoping to making new friends this year. I just don't want to see you sitting home waiting for Laura to call."

"I'm not against new friends, but Laura is my best friend," I said, a bit huffier than I intended. "And she's just busy getting ready to try out for the musical. They wanted to practice tonight. That's all."

"I'm just saying new friends can be a great part of middle school." Mom smiled to herself. "I remember when Christiane Larken moved to my town in seventh grade. She was so quiet in class. I thought she was stuck-up."

"Stuck-up?" I repeated. Mom used such funny phrases sometimes.

"Yes, but your grandmother said to give her a chance. *Maybe she's shy,* I remember her saying, and it turned out she was right. I invited Christiane to sit with me at lunch, and the rest is history. Ask Aunt Chris. She'll tell you the story."

"Aunt Chris is Christiane Larken?" I said in surprise. Aunt Chris lived in Massachusetts, so we didn't see her often, but when they got together, they talked for hours. Sometimes when they were on the phone, Mom laughed so hard I thought she would fall over. It wasn't hard to see how well they got along.

Mom nodded. "Yes. We've been friends ever since. Turns out she was terrified of starting a new school. That was why she was quiet. You never know what is going on in someone else's head. I'm just asking you to try to be present, get your head out of your phone, and look around. You might be missing out on an amazing friendship right in front of you." She kissed my head and closed the door behind her when she left.

I knew Mom meant well, but she was wrong. So was Taryn. Laura and I had been best friends for years. That didn't just end in a day. I just had to work on being cooler and liking some of the new activities she did. Maybe if I did that, she wouldn't keep ditching me for the drama queens. Or she'd invite me to hang out with them too. I wasn't sure I liked that idea, but if it meant hanging with Laura, it was worth it. I looked at my phone again. The sleepover picture was still open in that app. I'd captioned the picture *two peas in a pod*. We weren't anymore.

Then I noticed something I hadn't seen before. Just like on Instagram, this app had a like button and a comment feature. But this app also had a third option: a back arrow. What was that for?

I clicked on the button. Suddenly there was a bright camera flash, as if I had taken a picture, but no new image appeared on the screen.

This app doesn't even work. How lame.

I placed my phone down on my bedside table, and the next thing I knew, I was asleep.

⁓

"Zoooooeeeeee! ZOE!"

I felt someone shaking me, and I opened my eyes. Loud music was playing and I heard people laughing. The smell of burnt popcorn filled the air. I blinked hard. Was that Laura leaning over me?

"Don't go to sleep! It's only ten o'clock! We were just taking pictures! Wake up! Wake up! Wake up!"

I was so confused. "What are you doing here?" I asked with a yawn.

Laura started to laugh so hard she snorted. "What am I doing here? This is my house!"

What? I looked down. I was in my purple sleeping bag. Laura was in her purple sleeping bag. I looked up again. We were in her basement. I could see other girls stretched out on sleeping bags all around us, and a rom-com playing on the TV. This all felt very familiar. . . . .

Wait a minute!

This felt familiar because it *was* familiar! This was the sleepover Laura had! But it couldn't be. I had to be dreaming. Yes, that was it. I was dreaming about the sleepover because I'd just looked at the picture in that strange app.

Laura was looking at me. I tried to remain calm as I cleared my throat and spoke. "What day is it?"

"Saturday." Laura said, and started scrolling through her phone.

"No, I mean the actual date."

Laura snorted. "I don't know! June something."

"June?" I repeated, my heart beating fast. "You mean it's not the first day of school?"

Laura raised her right eyebrow and put down her phone. "Nooooo, it's the *last* week of school. School ends next Friday, you weirdo."

I sat up, my heartbeat feeling too fast. "Are you sure?"

It was a dream. That's what it was. A really vivid dream.

And whenever I had one of those—like that bad dream when I was getting chased by a clown—I pinched myself hard and woke up. I squeezed two pieces of my skin together and pinched myself. It hurt, but I was here. I pinched myself again. Laura was still staring at me. My mouth suddenly went dry, and the room felt like it was spinning. "Pinch me," I instructed Laura.

"You're not having a bad dream about clowns! You're awake!" Laura was laughing like she'd drunk too much soda, which on sleepovers, she usually did.

"I just want to be sure! Pinch me!"

"Fine!" Laura reached over and pinched my hand hard.

"Ow!" I screamed so loud the other girls looked over.

I was here.

In Laura's house.

At a sleepover that had happened months ago.

"How is this even possible?" I whispered. My mouth felt chalky.

"The sleepover?" Laura replied, going back to her phone again. "Mom said I couldn't do anything fun like take everyone to that new rock-climbing place, but she said I could still have people over." She looked at me worriedly. "You think it's going okay, right?"

I thought back to the arrow I had clicked on that app. Was it a redo button?

I heard a whooshing sound in my ears. I had to be absolutely positive this was real. "So you're saying we're still in sixth grade? Not seventh? And summer hasn't happened yet?"

"Um, yes . . ." Laura looked at the other girls. "Someone get Zoe a Coke. She needs caffeine because she's losing it!"

I grabbed my phone, which was in my sleeping bag next to me. I checked the date: It was June 21. Not September 6. This . . . this was so weird. But to my surprise I wasn't panicking. Should I have been panicking?

Then I remembered that the app was still on my phone. I clicked on the icon, and the picture of Laura and me at the sleepover came right up. This time it had a filmy pink haze over it. I tried to scroll, but the app was frozen. Who cared? I didn't need it anymore. I was getting my second chance!

I screamed at the top of my lungs, and one of the drama queens jumped.

"What is wrong with you?" Laura asked, but she was laughing.

I hugged her. "Nothing is wrong! Absolutely nothing has even gone wrong *yet*!" I started giggling uncontrollably now too. This was crazy, but it was real. "Tonight is going to be amazing! I can't wait to take more pictures!"

This was my chance for a retake.

CHAPTER SEVEN

Laura's basement smelled like a mix of floral detergent from the washing machine churning quietly in a large closet and cinnamon toast, which the twins ate all day long. It had been months since I'd been down here, and I'd really missed it. I'd missed us. I had to get this moment exactly right.

I tried not to look panicked. *Be present,* I could hear Mom saying. I put my phone back in the sleeping bag. It had been so warm to the touch it was practically pulsing, but I was still here. I turned to Laura, both of us still half in, half out of our sleeping bags. "Bring me up to speed. What have we done so far tonight since, um, I've been sleeping?"

Laura gave me an odd look. She was wearing her favorite *Hamilton* T-shirt, and her blond hair was pulled up into a messy bun. "Well, you brought Taryn's makeup and said we should do makeovers—she's going to kill you for that, by the way—but the other girls have way more makeup than we do, so they weren't interested."

"Yeah, I don't know why I did that," I said. "Who needs help with makeup when you have YouTube, right? All the tutorials are right there. I now know how to make our lashes triple long with this one mascara. It's to die for."

Laura looked sort of surprised. "Wow. Will you show me?"

"Maybe," I said coolly. See? I could be chill. "Have we eaten ice cream yet?" Laura shook her head. "Good. Because we should scratch that idea, too, even though, um, I made my dad stop to buy all the supplies." I felt a bit guilty about that part. "Making your own sundaes is kind of babyish."

Now Laura looked hurt. "I love ice cream."

"Me too," I said quickly, "but I feel like, isn't someone here lactose intolerant? Or is it gluten-free? Doesn't matter. We don't want anyone to feel bad." I distinctly remembered Ava shutting down my ice cream bar the first time, with the declaration *I don't do dessert.* I was just trying to save Laura—and myself—the humiliation. "Let's forget about the snacks and just hang out."

"Yeah, okay." Laura smiled. "I like that idea." She leaned over and hugged me. "I'm so relieved! I thought you'd push to do both those things or just sit in the corner with Reagan and Jada, trying to figure out why our urban, green space model came in third place at regionals."

"Me?" I shook my head. "No, I'm all about hanging out with . . . everyone." Well, really just Laura, but I needed to sound like a team player.

"Good! Because I want you to get to know everyone." Laura motioned to the other side of the room where Jada and Reagan were making lanyard bracelets and talking. "Unlike those two who just want to talk about Future City." She clutched her *L* necklace. "None of the girls from the musical are in the club, so I'd rather not talk about how we used to be in it."

"Used to?" I repeated, cautious.

Laura slid the *L* charm up and down the chain. "I don't know if I'm going to do it in seventh grade. I don't want people thinking I'm . . ." She trailed off, looking torn. "I don't know. Are you doing it?"

Was being in Future City like putting a nerd stamp on your forehead? I thought using the SimCity computer program to come up with all these awesome ideas to change urban development and help the environment was cool. And Ms. Pepper always said if we stuck with the club through high school, it would look great on our college applications. Some people even got scholarships. My parents were always going on to Taryn about scholarship potential already. But if Laura thought the club was lame, maybe I had to rethink things too. "I'm probably not doing it either," I said, and there was that chalky taste in my mouth again.

Laura, however, looked relieved. "I thought it was just me, Zo-Zo. Wait till I tell my mom that you're not doing it in seventh grade either! We really are so alike. You are the best friend ever." She leaned in and hugged me.

I squeezed hard and blinked back tears as I tried to remember this moment. "I try to be," I said softly. Tonight I was a whole new Zoe, even if I felt uncomfortable in her skin. I cleared my throat. "I mean, I am, and you better not forget it."

Laura shook her head. "Who are you, and what have you done with my best friend?"

I laughed. *She's still here, and she's ready to fight for our friendship.*

Laura pulled me in close again for a selfie. "Say 'sleepover'!"

"Sleepover!" I shouted, and waited for the flash. This was our retake. We would have a new picture to remember tonight with. Everything was about to change.

Ava jumped in front of us as the flash went off.

"Sleepover selfie!" she cheered, sloshing her soda over my sleeping bag. Laura and I jumped out of the way, sliding out of our sleeping bags to avoid the spill.

I'll be honest: I was not an Ava Sinclair fan. I knew I had to try with these girls for Laura's sake, but Ava seemed to deserve the drama queen nickname. Anytime I saw her, she was making a snarky comment about someone or rolling her eyes, and she was a bit bossy. The first time we were here she had decided everything, from whose sleeping bag would be placed where, to what movie we were watching and what game we played. I had to find a way to stop her from suggesting Truth or Text again.

Ava grabbed Laura's phone. "Eww. I don't like this shot at all. Retake!" I heard a swooshing sound as Ava deleted our picture.

Nooo! I swallowed hard and resisted the urge to snatch the phone from Ava. Now how would we get our new-and-improved selfie? We needed a good moment from tonight to make things right between us.

Didn't we?

I wasn't sure how the mystery app worked. Did we take a new picture and the old one disappeared with me along with it? Or did I have to redo every moment from now till the first day of seventh grade again to change our friendship? If that was true, I had another three weeks of Civil War reenactments ahead of me. Or not. Maybe there was a button in the app that took me right back to the present. I hadn't actually looked at the app too closely before I pressed that back arrow button.

There was a way to get back, wasn't there?

My hands were clammy as I pulled my phone out of my sleeping bag and slipped it into my pocket. The phone still felt warm. I needed to find a moment to look at the app without everyone asking about it. Maybe there were directions I hadn't noticed before.

Ava held Laura's phone and spun around looking for the best angle for a photo, her long, sleek black hair swishing back and forth as she moved. "The lighting is so bad down here!"

"So bad," Laura agreed.

I looked up at the lights. They seemed bright enough, but I nodded anyway. It felt like the thing to do.

Ava's friend Hyacinth, who towered over all the girls at six feet one inch, walked over holding a bowl of pretzels. "What are you guys doing?"

"Finding the right spot for a sleepover selfie." Ava stood on the couch and smiled at herself from three different angles. "No. This isn't good either. Hy, put down the pretzels and help me move this chair. Maybe if we move the sleeping bags over . . ."

"Good idea!" Laura kicked our sleeping bags away.

Reagan appeared behind me. "What are they doing?"

"Finding the perfect spot for a selfie," I said, and the two of us started to giggle. Laura and Ava shot us nasty looks, so we quickly stopped.

"Talk about spontaneous," Jada said as the others pushed a chair across the floor and it made a loud screeching noise. She nudged Reagan. "See? This is why I rarely post."

Reagan threw up her hands. "Here we go again!"

"I'm serious," Jada said. "You can't actually live the moment if you're not in it. Life is more than just a picture."

"You sound like my mom," I said.

Jada paled. "Is that bad?"

"No," I said, because the truth was they both had a point. Life was more than pictures, but I still liked posting. "No one should spend twenty minutes finding the right angle for a picture." Behind us, some of the girls were moving the couch. Dianne was going to flip.

Jada smiled shyly. "I agree. Hey. Did your mom sign you up for volleyball sleepaway camp this summer? My mom signed me up for week four."

"I wanted to go, but we're going on a three-week summer road trip," I explained.

"Bummer," Jada said.

"I know," I agreed. "Camp sounded fun. All of us sleeping in the same cabin, playing volleyball, telling ghost stories, and learning how to paddleboard? What's not to like?"

"I love paddleboarding!" Reagan's eyes lit up. "Hey. Wouldn't it be cool if we could design a lake in our next Future City design so people could paddleboard to work?"

Jada made a face. "Yeah, I don't see people in suits on paddleboards. But ooh! Maybe kayaks?"

"Or a clean-energy ferry service to cut down on cars?" I suggested, getting into the idea myself.

Jada squeezed my arm. "Yes! I love that! What about a city with no cars? All bikes?"

"Ooh . . . Ms. Pepper would like that!" Reagan agreed.

I felt my stomach relax. Talking with them didn't feel like work, like chatting with the other girls did. I didn't care about the perfect selfie angle or pranking boys. But I couldn't just stand here and talk to Jada and Reagan. I had to concentrate on Laura. *Focus, Zoe. Stop getting sidetracked and help Laura move the furniture.*

By the time I turned around, the girls had already moved the couch and two chairs out of the way and were arranging pillows while Ava watched. Sarah sat in the middle of all the pillows like a test model.

Stephanie Samuels, a girl I knew from English class, held up a rainbow-colored sleeping bag. "Whose is this?"

"Mine," Reagan said, her cheeks turning slightly red.

Steph glanced at Ava, who nodded. "Can we leave it out of the picture? It doesn't really . . . go with the others." Laura looked away.

"Sure," Reagan said, but I could tell she was embarrassed. Did a rainbow-colored sleeping bag scream sixth grade? I liked rainbows.

"Pile the pillows up high," said a girl with red hair. I remembered her name was Marisol Tolman. "It will be the perfect backdrop." Everyone spent another few minutes arranging the picture.

"I like it!" Ava said when everyone was finished. "Let's get in the shot."

The girls climbed over one another to get into view

while Ava looked at the setup on Laura's phone. Reagan, Jada, and I squeezed in beside the others.

"No. this isn't working. There's too many of us now. We'll look too tiny in the picture." Ava looked at Hyacinth, who nodded. "Um . . . let's take two pictures. One with half of us and then one with the other half."

"Laura!" I heard her mom yelling from the top of the stairs. "You better not be moving my couch down there!"

Laura's eyes widened, and she jumped up. "I'll be right back. Don't move anything!"

"Take a trial pic while she's gone," Hyacinth suggested. She held Laura's phone out to Reagan and Jada. "Can one of you take it?"

"Sure," Reagan said.

"I'll go in the second shot too." Jada stepped out of the setup, leaving me with the others. I hesitated, unsure if I should leave or stay.

"Okay, uh, say 'selfie'!" Reagan said.

"Selfie!" we shouted.

Laura hurried back down the stairs. "Guys, we've got to put the furniture back before my mom comes down here. She'll freak!"

I did not want Dianne getting mad. She could send everyone home before the party even really got started. A new selfie with Laura, it seemed, would have to wait.

CHAPTER EIGHT

"What should we do now?" asked Steph.

Once the furniture was back in place, we'd all sat down on our sleeping bags and looked at our phones for a while and lost track of time.

"Something quiet." Laura still looked pale. I had a feeling Dianne had gotten mad at her, and Laura just wasn't saying.

"I've got an idea!" Ava sat up on her pink plaid sleeping bag. "Let's play Truth or Text!"

"Oh, I love Truth or Text," said Marisol, slipping into place beside Ava before Sarah could get there. The other girls crowded around a table while Laura, Jada, Reagan, and I looked confused.

How were we back to this game again? Other moments from tonight had already changed. Why had this one stayed the same? It was almost as if history was fighting back.

"What's Truth or Text?" Jada asked, and I noticed two of the drama queens shooting each other a look.

Ava leaned forward, her green eyes bright. "It's Truth or Dare, but the dare is done by text. I ask a question, and you can either answer truthfully or text someone something on a dare."

"What kind of *something*?" Reagan asked.

Ava pursed her lips instead of saying more, and I felt my heart flutter, knowing what was coming. "Whatever we decide."

"It's so much fun," gushed Marisol.

"The most fun," agreed Steph.

It was not fun. The first time we were here, Laura wouldn't fess up a truth, so she had to text Jake Graser and tell him she liked him. He never replied, and Laura somehow blamed me for what happened. I needed to warn her, but if I pushed hard not to play the game, Laura might think I was scared. There had to be another option.

As Ava wrote out numbers to decide what order we would go in, I pulled Laura aside. "This sounds fun, but if your mom comes down and hears us playing this game, she is going to flip."

"I know." Laura sounded worried too. "But what am I supposed to tell Ava? I don't want her to get annoyed and not want to hang out with me anymore." She pursed her lips. "We're just going to have to watch the basement door for signs of my mom."

"That sounds risky," I said.

"Laura, are you playing?" Ava called to us. She held out the bowl with the numbers that would decide our order. "You don't have to pick because it's your house. You automatically go last. Zoe, your turn." I stared at the bowl worriedly and Ava looked from me to Laura. "Is there a problem?"

Laura looked flustered and turned to me. "Yeah, is there a problem?"

"Are you kidding?" I asked loudly. "Taryn and I play this all the time. I'm in." I pulled a number—I got second to last—and sat down right next to Ava. My heart started to pound. I had to think of a way to stop Laura from texting Jake.

"Great! Okay, Reagan, pick a number," Ava said.

Reagan lifted her chin defiantly. "We're not playing." Jada nodded, and the two of them dragged their sleeping bags over to a far corner. I watched them, impressed. I didn't remember Reagan bowing out the first time.

"Whatever, *babies,*" I heard Ava say under her breath, and Hyacinth snorted. "Okay, Hy. You picked the first number. Truth or text?"

"Truth," Hyacinth said, as if it should have been obvious.

Ava looked at Steph, who nodded. "Where do you get your hair cut?"

Hyacinth's face paled. "Um . . . at a salon?"

"What salon?" Stephanie pressed, already starting to giggle.

"BOGO Cuts." Hyacinth self-consciously touched her bangs. I didn't think they looked bad, but the other girls started laughing. "It's not a big deal. I only trim my hair like twice a year, and my mom likes a bargain." The girls laughed harder. Hyacinth shoved a handful of pretzels into her mouth to avoid saying anything else.

The questions were getting ugly. "Should we tell your mom to bring down that karaoke machine she got at work?" I whispered to Laura. She shook her head. "Are you sure? We . . ."

Laura turned to me, annoyed. "I said no. Leave it, Zoe."

Everyone looked at me. I felt like I'd been slapped. I sat back and listened to Steph go next.

"I'm not telling you what size jeans I wear!" Steph declared.

"Fine. Then text Emily Brandwine and tell her she has fish breath," Ava said.

"Noooo." Stephanie threw herself backward onto someone's pillow. "That's too mean!"

"You chose text!"

Steph sighed and got out her phone. "Fine. But I'm telling her when she texts back that my younger brother had my phone." I heard the whoosh as she hit send, and some of the girls cheered.

Laura was three turns away, and I was starting to sweat. Marisol chose truth and had to spill details about her first kiss with Stephen Corea. Had all the drama queens kissed boys already? I looked at Laura listening with rapt attention. She couldn't wait for her first kiss, but I wasn't sure I was ready. And I definitely wasn't ready for Laura to have to text Jake again. How did I turn this game around? Suddenly I had an idea. I jumped up right as Ava was about to go. "I've got to use the bathroom. Be right back." No one even looked at me.

I ran up the stairs and found Paige and Petra in the kitchen. I could hear Dianne on the phone in the other room—most likely with my mom, so I talked fast.

"Just the two I wanted to see." I leaned my elbows on the counter. "What are you guys doing right now?"

"Making the world's most gooey popcorn," Paige said as she drizzled way too much chocolate sauce onto a bowl of popcorn.

"Then we're going to post a video on YouTube and show everyone how to make it." Petra dumped almost a container full of sprinkles into the bowl.

I felt ill just looking at it. "Cool!" I said. "But you know what would be even cooler? If you did karaoke with us."

Paige blinked. "Mom said not to bother you guys."

"And Laura threatened not to speak to us till 2025 if we *did* bother you guys," Petra added. "That feels like a long time." Paige nodded in agreement.

I thought harder. "Would you do it if Laura and I took you to Melted Cookie next time we go? My treat."

Paige's brown eyes lit up. "Really?"

"I love Melted Cookie!" Petra screamed, and I shushed her.

We all loved Melted Cookie. What was not to like about an ice cream shop that let you pick your favorite ice cream flavor to sandwich between two warmed cookies? We didn't go often because both our moms thought seven dollars and fifty cents was a lot for an ice cream, but desperate times called for desperate measures.

Who knew going back in time would be so pricy?

"We will go, but here is what you have to do . . . ," I said.

By the time I finished negotiating and got back downstairs, it was my turn. I just hoped the twins were good at telling time.

"Look who is back," Sarah said. "You're up, Zara."

"It's Zoe." I sat down cross-legged next to Laura, who was spinning her rope bracelet around and around her wrist nervously. "And I'm ready."

Sarah grinned. "Truth or text?"

Last time I answered truth and had to tell everyone whether I'd already gotten my period (yes), and where I was when it happened (at volleyball practice). It was time to switch things up. "Text!"

Everyone oohed.

"Impressive." Ava gave me a high five. "No one has said text right off the bat. What are you hiding, Zoe?"

Oh, I don't know. Just that an app took me back in time to this sleepover so I could save my friendship? "Nothing. I'll text anyone you want. Go for it." I leaned forward, waiting.

Hopefully, by morning, I'd be gone. But *how* I got there and when I went back to, I wasn't sure. Did I go home to the minute I changed things and fade into oblivion right in front of their eyes? Or wake up back in my own bed like I had woken up next to Laura here? Did I still actively have to take another picture with Laura, which hadn't happened yet? I really should have looked to see if that app had an FAQ section.

"Zoe? Did you hear me?" Sarah asked.

"What? No. Sorry!" I held up my phone. "Who am I texting?"

Sarah smiled. "You have to text someone you're scared of and tell them exactly how you feel about them."

"Done!" I started typing immediately. This was an easy question. Why had I been worried?

ME: Hope you won your vball game today. Sorry I didn't come. I wish we were closer. I could really use my big sister sometimes. XO.

I held up the phone and showed the others.

"You texted your sister?" Ava looked disappointed.

I shrugged. "You said text someone I'm scared of, and I'm scared of Taryn. Big-time."

"So am I," Laura agreed, having my back.

For a second, I feared that Ava was going to say it didn't count, but instead, she looked impressed. "Smooth."

"Thanks," I said, feeling satisfied.

Paige and Petra came running downstairs, right on time. "Who wants to do karaoke?" Paige yelled.

Hyacinth jumped up. "You have a karaoke machine?"

"I love karaoke!" Marisol said. "Does it have every artist? Who wants to sing Taylor Swift with me?"

"I do!" said Hyacinth.

"Me too!" I stood up, happy to see that the drama queens were excited about the machine. This meant Laura wouldn't have to play Truth or Text. At least I'd gotten one thing right tonight.

"You want to sing?" Laura asked incredulously.

"Why not?" I said since Ava was still watching me. "I will if you will."

"We all will after Laura goes," Ava said. "Everyone playing the game has to take a turn."

"But karaoke is calling!" I tried, rushing to get the machine from the girls and plugging it in. The machine roared to life, sending rays of blue, pink, and yellow lights flashing across the basement ceiling.

"It's only fair," Ava said. "Truth or text, Laura?"

Laura looked at me worriedly.

"Truth!" I suggested.

Laura shifted in her seat uncomfortably. "No way."

I was starting to sweat. She had to change her mind. She had to! "Come on!" I nudged her right shoulder. "Truth is easy, I swear!"

"Zoe!" Laura snapped. "Let me decide. Seriously."

Hyacinth snorted. I shut up, feeling stupid.

Laura exhaled. "I'm picking text."

I paled as the other girls gathered around. I knew what came next. Disaster. Tears. Doom.

Ava thought for a moment. "Great. Text the boy you like."

"The boy I like?" Laura repeated, turning pink.

I couldn't just stand there and watch this go down again. "She doesn't like anyone."

"Not true!" Ava moved in closer. "She likes Jake Graser!"

"No, I don't," Laura said, but she stumbled over her words, making it all the more obvious.

"Jake is cute," Marisol agreed. "Tell him!"

"I don't like him!" Laura insisted, but her cheeks were so red, everyone knew she was lying.

"You chose text." Hyacinth shrugged. "Now text him. That's how the game works."

"Karaoke! Karaoke!" Paige cheered in the background. The lights on the machine brightened and spun, blinding Laura in the eyes.

This was like experiencing déjà vu. I'd lived this moment once before. After the girls finished hounding Laura to send the text, Sarah would pull Laura's phone out of her pocket and threaten to text for her. I felt a whooshing sound in my ears as I watched Sarah do just that. "Wait!" I cried. "Laura can't text Jake." Laura looked at me. I could see the fear in her eyes. It was time to take one for the team. "She's not the one who likes him. I am."

"*You* like him?" Steph repeated.

"Yes." Shakily, I grabbed Laura's phone from Sarah's sweaty hand. "So if anyone is going to text Jake about liking him, it's me." I quickly found Jake's name—Laura had his name in her phone forever, not that she'd ever texted him before—and I wrote him a text before I could second-guess myself.

Laura: My friend Zoe really likes you!

I hit send. The girls all shrieked. I looked at Laura, but I couldn't read her expression. She looked relieved . . . and yet kind of not. Reagan and Jada were watching from the corner of the room, and I wondered what they were thinking. I was proud of myself. I'd stopped Laura from being humiliated. I had been cool and played the game well. And I had taken the fall for Laura. Who cared what Jake thought of the text? It's not like I actually liked him. Laura knew that. This was a win. I half expected to disappear on the spot.

"Wow, I had no idea you had it in you, Zoe." Hyacinth high-fived me. "I can't believe you just did that."

Steph was still staring at the phone. "I wonder what he'll say! Wait! There's text bubbles." The girls crowded around Laura's phone. "Wait for it!"

"Zoe, come sing a Taylor song with me." Ava pulled me over to the karaoke machine.

"One sec!" I spun around, looking for Laura. She was standing in front of the doorway to the boiler room, next to the closet with the washer and dryer. I rushed over. The washer was loud. "Hey," I whispered. "I hope that was okay. I had to improvise, but I didn't want them knowing you—"

Laura whirled around. She was crying. "You like Jake Graser too? How could you do this to me?"

I jumped back in surprise and heard the washer hit the spin cycle. "I don't! I swear! I only said that so they wouldn't know you like him."

"Now he thinks you like him instead of me!" Laura hissed.

"He doesn't even know who I am!" I insisted as the spinning sound increased. "This is ridiculous! You *know* I don't like him, Laura. I was trying to help you."

Laura took deep gulping breaths. "I can't believe this. I really can't believe it. You're supposed to be my best friend."

"I am your best friend!" My heart started to beat fast again, and my mouth was dry. How had this spiraled out of control? "Laura, I swear on every secret ever told in the tree house—I don't like Jake Graser, okay?"

There was a scream from the other end of the room.

"Jake wrote back!" Steph shouted. "He said 'Do you mean Zoe Mitchell? She's cute'!" The girls screamed again. Reagan bit her lip.

Laura locked eyes with me. She looked so hurt that I couldn't breathe. The expression was quickly replaced with one of anger. "Thanks, Zoe. I hope you're really happy together." She brushed past me.

"Laura, wait. No!" I reached for her arm, but she pulled out of my reach. I heard Taylor Swift's voice fill the room.

"Zoe! Come on!" Ava yelled. "Sing with me!"

This was all wrong. I didn't want things to end this way! I needed to fix this, but how? Could I go back to tonight and try it again? Yes. I'd just start over. I pulled my phone out of my pocket. It was still warm to the touch. I walked into the boiler room and quietly closed the door, then pulled up the app. The picture of Laura and me at the sleepover was there, but there was a filmy pink haze over it. The app seemed to be locked on the photo, and the back arrow button was missing. What did that mean? *Please let me have another do-over. Please!* I closed my eyes.

"I wish I could start over and retake this picture again," I told the universe, hoping that saying the words out loud would make them come true.

Nothing happened.

Taylor hit the first chorus, and the girls' voices only grew louder.

"Zoe, come on already!"

I opened my eyes. I was still there. No. No. No. No!

I looked at the picture again, feeling panicked. Why wasn't this working? Couldn't I do the same memory over twice? What if I couldn't? I couldn't be stuck here! Laura hated me!

I kept tapping the faded picture over and over, then closed the app and reopened it. Miraculously, it finally clicked over to my feed. All of my pictures—even ones I hadn't posted—seemed to be uploaded to the app now. There was the picture of my lobster dinner, and Taryn and me on a battlefield with some soldiers from a reenactment, and even the selfie I'd just taken on my bed before I discovered the app. At least that would take me back to the present. If this app still worked.

"Zoe!" I heard my name being called again, and panicked.

I clicked the back arrow on the picture of me on my bed and immediately saw a giant flash, just like I had the first time. Then I blinked and was gone.

CHAPTER NINE

When I opened my eyes, my phone was still in my hand. All I heard was silence. And snoring.

Taryn.

She snored louder than a freight train. I could always hear her, even though she was a room away.

I sat up and looked around. It was dark, but I could see the outline of the mirror on my closet door, and the pictures I had taped on it.

I unlocked my phone and quickly checked the date: September 6. I'd made it back! I threw my head back on my pillow and exhaled slowly.

Either that was the craziest dream I ever had or that app really worked.

I hit the home button on my phone and the screen cast a warm glow over my bed. Then I started scrolling through the pages of apps I had (most of which I didn't even use). At some point, I'd even downloaded Fake-a-Tan Filters.

And then there it was, the glowing fluorescent pink icon.

The Retake app was real.

I screamed into my pillow to keep from waking up the entire house. How could this be? Did other people have this app too? And how did it wind up on my phone? I still didn't understand how the app worked or why it had appeared, but I was never letting this phone out of my sight—this was my way to fix things!

I opened the app and searched through my feed for the picture of Laura and me in our sleeping bags from the original sleepover. It felt like I was scrolling forever. There were so many pictures I didn't even remember taking! Finally, I found one from the weekend before school ended this past spring.

Huh.

That was weird.

The picture of Laura and me at the sleepover was gone.

Instead, it had been replaced with the picture of me with the drama queens that Laura wasn't even in. My heart started to pound. Was this really the only picture we took that night? It looked like Ava had posted this photo, and then I'd reposted it with Ava's original hashtag, #sleepoverprepwiththeog.

"OG"? I wasn't part of their group.

Below the picture were comments. Laura's was first. It was a kissy-face emoji.

That was a good sign. If Laura was using the kissy-face emoji, then she couldn't still be mad at me about the Jake Graser text! I must have explained what happened and all was forgiven.

I read the other comments: Steph had written *So hot* and Ava had written *BFFs!* Even Hyacinth had commented on my post, writing *best night ever!* So I guess things between us had improved from there. Was I part of their group now?

My eyes felt so heavy, I could barely keep reading without the words on the screen starting to swim. But I felt happy. Maybe Laura and I were our old selves again and I didn't even need to go back to that night. But if we weren't—I yawned so wide it seemed to crack my jaw—I could just click on this picture in the morning and start all over again.

———

"Zo-Zo! Wake up!"

"So tired," I mumbled, turning away from the offending voice.

"Come on, Zoe Golightly. You're going to be late."

"Zoe Golightly"?

Only Taryn called me that, and it had been years since she'd done so. Back when we were in this *Breakfast at Tiffany's* phase, we called each other Taryn Golightly and Zoe Golightly and spent every waking minute that rainy summer rewatching Audrey Hepburn movies. This was when Taryn actually talked to—rather than barked at—me. Come to think of it, it was the summer before she started middle school.

Middle school ruins everything.

I turned over, curious. Taryn was *smiling* at me.

Her smile quickly turned into a frown. Oh no.

Taryn thumbed a piece of the pale teal top she was wearing. It had a V-neck with tiny rope braiding across it. "Is it all right if I borrow this to wear today?"

Huh? I didn't recognize the top. We never shared clothes.

"It's not Ava's chosen color for Monday, is it?" Taryn asked.

Ava who? Ava what?

Taryn sat down on the edge of my bed. "Please? I swear I won't get anything on it. I won't even go out to lunch. It will be clean and back in your drawer tomorrow." She flashed me the dimple in her right cheek. "I'll even let you wear those ripped jeans you love so much."

"Really? Okay!" I didn't even remember buying this shirt, let alone wearing it. What was with the rope braiding? That didn't look like my style at all, but it fit Taryn perfectly.

Taryn jumped up, ran into her room, and came back with the jeans I coveted. "Here."

I pinched myself to make sure I wasn't dreaming. Nope.

"And hey, if you're not with Ava and Sarah and everyone tomorrow night, do you want to hang? We could get sushi and watch an Audrey Hepburn movie. You've been so busy, we haven't had a sister night in forever."

Okay, now I really knew something was up. Taryn never wanted to hang out with me anymore. But who was I to refuse? "Sure!"

Taryn pulled back my quilt. "Now get up! Marisol's mom will be here any minute. I told Mom you were up fifteen minutes ago."

"Marisol?" I repeated. "Ava's friend?" Taryn nodded. "Don't I take the bus?"

Taryn turned to walk out the door. "Get dressed already before Mom changes her mind!"

"'Changes her mind'? About what? Where is Mom?" I asked.

Taryn whipped her head back to look at me with a raised eyebrow. "You sure you want to ask either of those questions? You're lucky she left early today, or she'd have been all over you about that stunt you pulled."

"What stunt?" I asked, but Taryn shook her head and kept going, waving her hand toward my corkboard, which I noticed was overflowing with pictures. There were pictures of me, Laura, and the drama queens at the beach, at an amusement park, holding a broken stop sign (um, wasn't that illegal?), on a campout, even onstage doing . . . karaoke? I was holding a microphone in the picture. No way.

There were no photos of Laura and me alone, but tons of us with her friends Ava, Hyacinth, Sarah, Steph, and Marisol. I didn't see Jada or Reagan in any of the pictures, though, or anything from Future City.

Clearly things had changed from that one party, but it looked like for the better. Taryn and I were hanging out, my photo board was full of fun I didn't remember having, and I no longer had to take the bus!

The second day of school was going much better than the first already.

I brushed my teeth, combed my hair, went back to my room to get dressed, pulling on Taryn's jeans—they were as perfect as I'd always imagined—and then I went to my closet to pick out a top. *Whoa!* Where did these new clothes come from? And when did I get so neat? My clothes were now coordinated by color and hanging on racks rather than littering the floor. I grabbed a blue button-down top with anchors on it. It looked really cute with the jeans.

A car honked.

"Your ride is here!" Taryn yelled.

"Coming!" I grabbed my bag and my phone. It felt warm, as if it had been working hard all night. I guess it had. I quickly texted Laura.

Me: Hey! See you in Mr. Goran's class. Avoid a seat in the spit zone!

I waited a second for Laura's reply, but none came. Maybe she was in the car with Marisol already. As soon as I stepped outside, I saw a red minivan parked in the driveway. The sliding door opened and Marisol poked her head out. "Get in!"

I climbed in and came face to face with five girls wearing yellow. Laura wasn't one of them.

Ava looked up from her phone and grimaced. "I thought we agreed on yellow today." She was wearing a yellow eyelet dress.

"We definitely said yellow," said Sarah, even though she didn't look up from her phone. She had on a yellow *The Lion King* T-shirt.

"Yellow!" said Hyacinth, holding up her wrist, which had a yellow scrunchie wrapped around it.

"Z, you were the one who suggested yellow in the first place," said Steph, who had a yellow headband in her hair. "And now you're wearing blue."

"Seat belt, Z!" said Mrs. Tolman, who clearly knew me and called me Z.

Ugh. Dad always joked Z would be my alien name. We always joked that we'd know if there had been an alien infiltration if anyone used Z as my real name. Now the drama queens were.

"Sorry, I must have forgot." I climbed into the third row next to Steph, and the door shut behind me. Ava and Hyacinth were sitting in front of me checking their Instagram feeds. "Where's Laura? Is she sick?"

Hyacinth snorted. "Laura," she said, but that really wasn't an answer.

None of the other girls replied. That's when I started to worry. Where was Laura? And why was I getting a ride to school and she wasn't? Not that I missed the bus, but this car was warm and smelled like a sea of perfumes that was making me gag. I had to calm down and figure out what was going on. I fished in my bag, hoping to find my metal water bottle. I found it and took a swig.

Marisol turned around in the front seat and smiled at me. "I'm wearing yellow *and* blue, so I guess Z and I think alike."

Sarah gave me a skeptical look. "Or maybe Z called you and told you she changed her mind." Everyone looked at me as I busied myself taking another chug. "That would be a best friend thing to do."

I spewed water all over Ava and Hyacinth.

"Eww!" Hyacinth cried.

"Z! What gives?" asked Ava.

"Marisol and I are best friends?" I barely knew her!

"Girls, you're *all* friends," Marisol's mom chimed in.

"Mom," Marisol hissed.

"Sarah's just paranoid." Ava wiped off the water with a tissue. "We equally adore each other." The others nodded. "I'm sure Z just forgot *she* suggested wearing yellow today." She smiled at me. "I'm sure she won't forget we're wearing gray tomorrow."

"Gray!" Marisol said, and texted herself a reminder.

I thought back to Laura's first-day-of-school picture when the drama queens were wearing rainbow-colored skirts. Did they color-coordinate so everyone knew they were friends? Why couldn't everyone wear what they wanted?

Mrs. Tolman pulled up in front of the school. "Have a great second day!" The side door slid open, and the drama queens began to pile out. "What time is Steph's mom getting you this afternoon? Are there play auditions yet, or is that next week?"

I froze climbing out of the minivan. Play auditions? I was part of the play now too?

"Next week," Hyacinth said. "But I think we're practicing at Sarah's this afternoon, then going for pizza."

Mrs. Tolman nodded. "Okay, text me if you need a ride." Then she was off.

Hyacinth winked at me. "Play practice and pizza *after* we go shopping at On Point. It's your turn to pick out what top we're buying!"

She said it like I had the money to shop in that store. I

didn't. On Point was a boutique in town where there was nothing under forty dollars. Even their scrunchies were designer and cost fifty dollars and up.

I searched the crowd for Laura, half expecting to see her waiting for us at the curb, but she wasn't there either. My phone buzzed in my bag, and I pulled it out, wondering if it was her texting me to say where she was. Instead, it was Mom.

> **Mom:** I hate fighting with you, but I meant what I said. Your attitude has to change. This is not like you.

Huh? Another text, much longer than the first, appeared.

> **Mom:** Lying about where you are, not answering texts, asking for money almost daily to buy frozen coffee drinks and all those clothes. We can't keep up with this spending! You want more money, start babysitting, but no, you don't want to miss out on a minute with your friends. Zoe, if this doesn't stop, you won't just be grounded; you won't leave the house again till high school graduation. And don't get me started on how you've been treating Laura.

How *I've* been treating Laura? Spending money on coffee drinks? I didn't even drink coffee! And what clothes?

Unless . . . Was that what Hyacinth meant by picking out shirts at On Point? Did the drama queens take turns deciding what clothes we bought? Why would I want all my clothes to look just like theirs? I would never do that . . . would I? I thought again about my new color-coordinated wardrobe. Obviously, things had changed. My heart started to pound as a third text appeared.

> **Mom:** I expect you home for dinner—do not go for pizza after school! Marisol's mom already texted me that's the plan—and we will talk further. I love you.

"Z! You coming?" Hyacinth and the girls were headed to the main entrance. Our two assistant principals were standing outside greeting students.

I scanned the crowd again for Laura. Where was she?

"Z! Let's go!"

I put my phone back into my pocket and hurried after the sea of yellow. Maybe the answers I was looking for were waiting inside.

CHAPTER TEN

The halls were crowded as Marisol and I zigzagged around people hanging out in front of their lockers. Before first period was the most chaotic time of the day at Fairview. I didn't see Reagan or Jada either. I tried looking for Laura, but it was no use. Eventually, I even lost sight of Marisol.

"Hey."

When I turned around, I came face to face with Jake Graser. "Hey?" Was he talking to me?

He held his books under one arm and balanced a Sharks lacrosse cinch bag over his left shoulder. "How have you been?"

"Good? I think?" It was an honest answer, but it still didn't explain why Jake was talking to me.

"Cool." He ran a hand through that floppy brown hair of his that always covered his right eye. I constantly teased

Laura that Jake needed a serious haircut. "You have math first, right?" he said. "Can I walk you up there?"

Walk me to class? *Me?*

I felt someone grab my hand. It was Marisol. "Sorry, Jakey, she's got to go." Marisol pulled me away and Jake just stood there looking sort of defeated. "He is so suffocating, am I right?" We bobbed and weaved our way through the crowd again and headed up the stairs. "I mean, you dumped him weeks ago, and he still hasn't gotten the hint."

"*I* dumped Jake Graser?" I stopped short, and two guys walking behind us crashed into me.

"Sorry, Z!" one guy apologized before walking away.

I didn't even know who they were and they were calling me Z? And I'd dated Jake Graser? No wonder Laura hadn't texted me back! No, this wasn't how things were supposed to go at all! My hands were starting to feel clammy. I could almost feel my phone burning in my jeans pockets—excuse me, *Taryn's* jeans pockets, because she liked me enough to lend them to me. Meanwhile, I was overspending money I didn't have and was in huge trouble at home. "I don't understand what is going on."

Marisol cocked her head to one side. "You really need to calm down. You'll never beat Sarah for the lead in *Charlie and the Chocolate Factory* if you get this worked up, and I'd prefer you get the part over her. No offense. Maybe I'll even get to be your understudy."

"I am not trying out for *Charlie and the Chocolate Factory*! I'd break out in hives if I had to do the play."

"Technically, it's a musical, but hey!" Marisol stopped and stood in front of me, her eyes burning into my head. "What have we talked about?"

"Uh . . ." I didn't know the answer to this question.

"Be confident!" Marisol said as if I should know. "You have to believe you'll get the part." She looped her arm through mine. "There's nothing to be scared of. All of us will be cheering you on when you're up there trying out. Besides, it will be fun. We already agreed we're doing the play together as a group."

For a moment I wasn't sure what to say. Marisol was being really nice. She made the drama queens sound like my own personal cheerleaders. Maybe that's what Laura liked about them. But at the end of the day, doing the drama—or musical—just wasn't what I was interested in. "Yeah, but . . ."

"Z . . ." Marisol played with the long yellow beaded necklace around her neck. "Everything okay? You were so quiet in the car this morning. Do you have food poisoning? Maybe the hibachi place had bad sushi. Ava keeps saying we have to try somewhere new since everyone goes there now, even Laura."

I grabbed Marisol by the shoulders. "Laura? Laura Lancaster? Where is she?"

Marisol looked alarmed. "How should I know? We haven't spoken to her in a while."

"'We'?" I echoed. "You mean you, right?"

"I mean all of us. You know things have been frosty since that sleepover at her house right before summer. First, Jake was all into you and she was jealous, and then you sort of took her spot in the group." She shrugged. "I guess she finally got tired of it because she fell off the radar by the time *Annie* rolled around. Things have calmed down, I guess, but she really hates you."

"Hates me?" A ringing sound started to whoosh through my ears. "Why?"

"Because . . . Uh-oh." Marisol's eyes widened. "Speaking of drama—there she is. . . ." She motioned down the hall.

Laura was walking alone, her head down, a *Charlie and the Chocolate Factory* script visible in her pile of books. Coincidentally, she was wearing the same vintage yellow *Lion King* shirt Sarah had on.

"I wouldn't talk to her if I were you," Marisol warned, but I was already running toward her. "Last time things didn't go so well."

"Laura!" I called frantically as people in the hallway turned to look at us. "Laura!"

Laura saw me and quickly turned on her track shoes.

But I wouldn't give up. "Laura!" She turned left into the

girls' bathroom, and I followed. I grabbed her before she could close herself into a stall.

Her face was eerily calm. "Oh, now you can talk to me when no one is around?" she said coldly, and I winced.

"It's not like that," I said, gulping for air.

"Let me guess—next, you're going to tell me you're sorry," Laura said, folding her arms. "Guess what? You're too late. I waited all summer for you to apologize, but you never did. You ghosted me, took my friends and the boy I liked, and acted like I didn't exist."

I never would have done that, would I? "Please. You're my best friend. That night at the sleepover with the Jake text . . . I was just doing it to protect you."

"Protect me?" Laura freaked. "You were looking out for yourself. I saw you trying to kiss up to Sarah and Ava, which is funny because you always told me they were drama queens!"

"You can have them back," I blurted out. "I don't want to be friends with them, audition for the play, overspend at On Point, or have to choose my outfit for school based on a group decision."

"Is that so?" I heard someone say.

I turned around. Marisol was standing in the doorway, and she actually looked hurt. Now I felt even worse.

"Find someone else to sit with at lunch," Marisol said.

"Wait, I . . ." But Marisol stormed away.

"Guess your friendship with them is over now too," Laura said.

I inhaled sharply and tried not to cry.

"Getting upset isn't going to work with me," Laura said coldly. "We both know you couldn't find your own life so you had to take mine. When we were friends I could never have anything for myself! You wanted everything—even Jake!"

Was that really what Laura thought? That I wanted her life? It wasn't true. I just wanted her to still be part of mine. "I swear you've got this all wrong. . . ."

How did one little text change so much?

"Let me make things right," I said desperately as the first bell rang. "I miss you. You're my best friend."

Laura looked unfazed. "If this is how you treat your best friend, you don't deserve one. In fact, I wish we'd never been friends to begin with. Stay away from me!" Laura ran out of the bathroom.

Before the door even swung shut behind her, I burst into tears. I didn't care that I was missing first period, or that I'd get detention. I couldn't face anyone like this. I wasn't sure how long I stood there crying before I heard a squeaky stall door open and footsteps.

"Zoe? Are you okay?"

It was Clare. When I saw her, I started to sob even harder.

"I didn't mean to eavesdrop. I was in a stall, and I heard

you two come in and start yelling and . . . oh geez, Zoe, I'm so sorry. Listen to me. Take a deep breath," she said, and I did as I was told. "Good." Clare wet a paper towel and handed it to me. "This will keep your face from getting blotchy. You don't want to go out in the hallway looking like you were crying. Even though, well, you were."

I pressed the wet towel to my face and felt my breathing start to slow. "Thanks." I stopped sniffling. "What are you doing in here anyway? No one uses this bathroom."

"I know. That's why I use it." Clare ran a hand through a strand of her purple-dipped hair. "Or at least that's why I did at first." She looked around at the peeling pink-painted walls. "Last year I was in here crying every day." She half smiled. "It feels like some unofficial rule that girls should always help another girl crying in the bathroom."

We laughed till the sound died out and I could hear a faucet leaking at one of the sinks. Someone needed to fix that ASAP. I looked curiously at Clare. "I don't mean to pry, but why did you cry so much last year?"

"It was over my best friend too," Clare said. "Ava Sinclair." I must have looked surprised, because then Clare said, "Yeah, a lot of people can't believe we were friends either. But Ava was different when we were both at Camp Elementary. Would you believe she lived for STEM Club? We even won a Long Island robotics competition for a LEGO MINDSTORMS robot we programmed."

"Ava?" I repeated. "Built LEGO robots for fun?" The girl who talked about nothing but boys and coordinating outfits was into building robots?

"We loved it. *I* still love it," Clare said, "but once we got here . . . Ava suddenly wanted to be someone else. More popular, I guess. She said robotics wasn't cool. And I guess I wasn't either."

Poor Clare. What happened to her was awful . . . and yet sort of familiar. "I'm sorry."

"Yeah, me too." Clare looked suddenly sad. "Sixth grade was rough. Ava either ignored me or took shots at me for liking robotics, and I spent most of the year in this bathroom wishing I could do things differently. . . ." She trailed off. "Anyway. I was in here a lot." She looked around. "And you know what I always wished this room had?"

"A TV and a couch?" I joked. "Because then I'd never leave."

Clare pulled away a piece of the peeling paint, revealing someone's graffitied name underneath. "Someone to vent to." Her face lit up. "I was at my cousin's school for a volleyball game once, and their girls' bathroom had a wall you could write notes to each other on."

I looked at the faded pink paint that reminded me of a bottle of Pepto-Bismol and imagined a wall of Post-it notes. "That does sound pretty cool."

"Yeah, people could leave messages for each other like 'It gets better, I swear,' and 'No friend is worth crying over this much.'" She and I both stared at the wall, clearly seeing the same possibility. "Maybe if I had been staring at notes instead of peeling pink paint I would have stopped crying about Ava sooner and moved on."

Move on. But I wasn't ready to do that. I went over to the dripping faucet and gave it a quick turn to tighten it. The drip stopped. It was nice to see something could be easily fixed. "You know, if you like STEM, I'm in a club called Future City. Reagan and Jada are in it too. We design eco-friendly cities. You should join."

Clare looked intrigued. "I didn't know the school had a Future City club."

"Yep! The first meeting should be in the next couple of weeks. You should come." I looked in the mirror at my blotchy face and pressed the wet towel to my cheeks again.

"Maybe I will," Clare said. "What about you and Laura? What are you going to do?"

"Try talking to her again." Even if I had to go back in time to do it. "Laura has been my best friend for years. I'm not about to give up on us yet."

Clare thought for a moment. "Then maybe you just need to remind her how good a friend you are. Get her to do something you both like."

When was the last time we had fun together? We both loved the water. But I couldn't go back to that day at the cabana when I threw her birthday party. Things went too wrong. I needed a day when things went right.

Instinctively, I pulled out my phone. It was so hot, it hurt my fingers. Was the app making my phone run hot? What if it fried my phone? I looked for the familiar pink icon and counterclockwise arrow and started scrolling through pictures. I couldn't quit now. I smiled. "I think I have an idea. Thanks for listening, Clare. And for your tip with the wet towel." It had been a while since I had someone to really talk to.

Clare was staring at my phone. "No problem. Guess we're both going to need late passes for math. Are you coming?"

"I'll be right behind you," I lied.

"Okay. I'll tell Ms. Brandle you had 'girl problems' and you're in the bathroom." Clare grinned. "That will buy you ten minutes."

I waited till I heard the door close.

It was time for another retake, which was a pretty cool name for an app, if I did say so myself. What if I somehow invented it and had no idea? I mean, was it impossible to think Future Me came back and put it on Present Me's phone? If that were true, then this app needed a name, and Retake was a perfect one.

I scrolled through pictures searching for a water-related way back into Laura's life. This reality was a bust. Mom and I were fighting, I had an ex-boyfriend I didn't even remember, and Laura couldn't stand me. The only good thing to come out of this was that Taryn and I were getting along again. I hated giving up our new relationship, but this wasn't working. From the outside I'm sure my life looked perfect—I was popular, I had great clothes, lots of friends—but I didn't want this. So where—or when—did I go to now?

And that's when I spotted it: a picture of Laura and me on the bus, on our way to Aquatopia. Sure, Dougie Hoffman had photobombed the shot with half his head, but this was clearly a picture of Laura and me having fun together. *On way to Aquatopia!* I had written. I had hashtagged the picture #bffmermaids. The photo was from our spring sixth-grade trip to an indoor water park. I remember Laura and I looked forward to that trip all year. Laura had been so busy with the sixth-grade play that we hadn't hung out in weeks. But that day, we sat next to each other on the bus and spent the whole ride singing and talking about all the rides we wanted to go on. We were going to spend the whole day together.

Except . . .

Laura had been kind of focused on finding a way to go on a ride with Jake. Even though they hadn't hung out, she was sure the water park would be a great way to get him to notice her. She made us follow him onto Paradise Plunge, which was a water slide with a sixty-foot drop and had an almost ninety-minute wait time. I didn't want to waste time on line when there was so much else to do, but Laura begged me. "We're right behind him!" she'd said. "He has to talk to me." And he did, which made Laura happy, till she got to the front of the line and he chivalrously offered to let her go first . . . and she panicked. I teamed up with Jake and tried to convince her to go on, but it wound up backfiring. Laura got embarrassed and said I had made a scene. We argued, neither of us went on the slide, and we spent the rest of the afternoon not talking to each other.

Okay, so the day wasn't perfect, but the field trip was the perfect chance to spend time with Laura. This time I would convince her to skip Paradise Plunge, stop worrying about Jake, and just enjoy going on the rest of the rides together. I'd tell her that she and Jake would talk when the time was right. Laura wouldn't get embarrassed, we wouldn't fight, and she'd see that I was the best friend ever.

Okay, Retake app, let's do this. My finger hovered over the back arrow button under the Aquatopia photo. I had no idea if saying the words out loud did anything, but it felt important. "I wish I could do this moment over and prove to Laura how awesome our friendship is." Then I clicked the button.

There was a bright camera flash, and then the bathroom surrounding me was gone.

CHAPTER ELEVEN

"Zoe! Wake up! We're almost there!"

When I opened my eyes, I was sitting on a crowded school bus wearing my bathing suit cover-up. Laura was seated next to me. *Yesssssss.*

I sighed contently. "Killer bees, it worked."

Laura stared at me. "Killer what?"

"Killer bees," I explained. "It's something you say now." Oh wait. She didn't say that yet, and maybe she never would because as of this moment, we hadn't had that awful sleepover at her house yet. She wasn't hanging out with the drama queens. Laura was on the field trip with me, and we were still best friends. I couldn't help but smile. So far so good.

"Nothing. I'm just excited."

Someone threw a ball over the seat we were sitting

in, and a boy a few rows in front of us caught it. One of the chaperones started yelling at him from the front of the bus.

"Sixth graders, I expect more from you!" said Mr. Bowen, our assistant principal. "We've only got fifteen minutes left of this bus ride. Let's try not to break a window." I had to strain to hear him over all the laughing and talking.

"Dude! Fifteen minutes till we finally get to experience the awesomeness of Paradise Plunge!" Dougie crowed. He had on a Sharks lacrosse pinnie and was wearing goggles that matted his long black hair, which was pulled into a ponytail.

"Technically, it will be longer than fifteen minutes, but whatever," said Jake. He raised a fist in solidarity. "Paradise Plunge!" A group of boys cheered.

"That ride is going to be epic!" Ava said from a seat a few rows behind me. Hyacinth let out a "Whoop-whoop." The two of them were wearing teal headbands. Behind them, Steph and Sarah were buried in their phones. One had on a teal scrunchie, the other a teal T-shirt. Marisol was directly behind them. She had on teal earrings.

Dougie lifted the goggles, which left rings around his brown eyes, and stared at us.

"Hey," I said, since things were kind of awkward with the staring and all.

He burped loudly and turned back in his seat.

Laura shuddered. "Ugh, he is such a Neanderthal." She turned to me. I could just make out the faded outline of the henna tattoo on her arm that she had gotten at the sixth-grade play wrap party. Sarah had gotten one too. It was the first time I remembered feeling like Laura was drifting away, even if she wasn't hanging out with the drama queens outside play practice yet. "Do you think we should go on Paradise Plunge with the boys?" she whispered.

"No way," I said, thinking fast. "Not after what happened to Peter Plover."

"What happened to him wasn't *that* bad." Laura shifted uncomfortably.

"He livestreamed his ride down Paradise Plunge. Puke in the tube and all." Once Peter was inside the tube, a door closed around him, and the three-second countdown completely freaked him out. Halfway down the tube, still streaming with his phone in a waterproof pouch, he puked all over the slide. They had to clear the slide area for two hours to clean it up. "I heard Pukey Pete is going to private school next year because this year was such torture." Laura's eyes were wide.

Okay, so maybe I was exaggerating, but I needed to really get the point across.

"Okay, that's really bad, but what if I get on line in front of Jake and say I'm scared to go on Paradise Plunge? Then he can talk me through it and we'll have a moment." Laura had a dreamy look on her face.

Time for some tough love. "Unless you chicken out and don't go down the slide. Then you'll worry Jake and his friends will call *you* the new Pukey Pete. We cannot let that happen." Laura's look of joy was quickly replaced with one of terror.

"Did you say Pukey Pete?" Dougie turned around again. "Are you going to throw up on Paradise Plunge?"

"Nope. Why would we want to go on that ride?" I answered for us. "I hear people lose their swim shorts on it all the time." Dougie's eyes widened, and he went back to his conversation.

Laura started to giggle. "That's not true, is it?"

I shrugged and started chuckling. "Who knows? But it sounded good! I just don't think you should go on a ride where you'll probably bail last-minute—no offense."

Laura pulled at her blond hair and sighed. "You know me so well."

Yeah, and I'd also already lived this day once before already. "But that doesn't mean we can't find other ways to get you in front of Jake so he can see how awesome you are."

"Like how?" Laura's face flushed.

She was probably wondering how I knew about boys and being cool all of a sudden. "Let me think for a moment."

"I will too," she said, and put her earbuds in. She immediately started humming a show tune.

I needed advice, but from who? It's not like anyone

besides me knew this day already happened once before. I needed to talk to someone who'd gone on this trip and survived without fighting with their best friend.

I needed Taryn.

I pulled out my phone, which seemed to only be getting warmer, and texted her.

> **Me:** Hey. On way to Aquatopia. You in class?
>
> **Taryn:** At lunch. What do you want?

Things were back to normal with Taryn at least.

> **Me:** I need advice.
>
> **Taryn:** YOU need MY advice?
>
> **Me:** Yes!!!
>
> **Taryn:** Seriously? OK. I'm just surprised. Usually the only one you listen to is Laura.

I remembered Taryn saying this to me the night we went for hibachi too. Could that be why Taryn and I didn't talk much anymore? Did she really think I only listened to Laura? I looked at my best friend, who was humming a show tune I didn't know.

> **Me:** Not true! This is actually about Laura.
>
> **Taryn:** Ahhh. That's why you want to talk to me. You can't talk to her!

I didn't want Taryn thinking that. The one thing I'd learned from my first retake was that being honest with Taryn brought us closer together.

Me: No, I always need you! You're my sister. I miss
talking to you and I could use your help here.
Taryn: Really?
Me: Yes. Really!

Taryn didn't answer right away, but hopefully, pouring my heart out would help her see that I missed us as much as I missed Laura. I stared at my phone, waiting for the text bubbles to appear. Finally, they did.

Taryn: 😊😊😊 Okay! I'm all ears. (Till lunch is over.)
Me: Yay! So I told Laura not to go on the Paradise
Plunge slide because she's going to freak out, but
she wants to impress Jake and I want to help her do
that. What do I tell her to do?
Me: Because you know I have zero experience with
boys.
Taryn: She doesn't either, you know.
Me: So what do I tell her???
Taryn: If she's scared, tell her to skip the Plunge
and follow Jake onto the lazy river instead. They
can float around talking to each other without being
interrupted or having to plunge down a death slide.

Me: Wow. That's a good idea.

Taryn: I know. I'm brilliant. Also, you should go on the Plunge without Laura. It's terrifying in the best possible way and you love that stuff.

Me: True, but today is about me and Laura.

Taryn: Even though she's trying to ditch you for a boy?

Me: I just want her to be happy.

Taryn: Very Hallmark.

Taryn: Look, you're a good friend, but it can't always be all about what Laura wants. If YOU want to go on the ride, go. If not, don't. Just don't waste your day doing everything for Laura. You've been dying to go on this trip.

She had a point. I hadn't really thought about what I wanted. Maybe that was the problem. Did I want to go on the ride? Not really. I wanted to go in the wave pool and on a four-person tube and the Venus Slydetrap, which everyone said reminded them of a toilet bowl because the raft went around and around, then dropped down what looked like a drain. Laura and I were so busy fighting the first time, I missed half the rides. *Fun. Concentrate on having fun,* I reminded myself.

Me: Thx for your help!

Taryn: NP. Now go away. I only have ten minutes left to eat my burrito.

The lazy river would be much better for Laura and Jake to have time together. And after she talked to Jake, she'd be so happy, we'd spend the rest of the day going on rides having the best time together. This plan was perfect.

I pulled out one of Laura's earphones.

"Here's what we're going to do: We'll wait for Jake to go on the lazy river and follow him on. You can float up next to him, and he will be so mesmerized by everything you have to say, he'll keep going around and around the river just to chat with you. And you don't have to worry about a sixty-foot plunge at all."

"The lazy river," Laura repeated, a small smile forming on her lips. "Why didn't I think of that? You're brilliant!"

Actually, Taryn was brilliant, but Laura didn't need to know that. "I truly am."

Laura held up her phone. "Let's take a selfie! I'll call it *on way to Aquatopia with bestie!*" I leaned into the picture's frame, and she snapped the shot.

"Bestie." I breathed a sigh of relief. We had a new photo of us looking happy. We had a plan to find Jake that would avoid Laura being embarrassed. And we had plenty of time now to go on fun rides and just catch up about everything and anything. Laura wouldn't even need to go looking for the drama queens. I smiled at the thought.

When we stepped off the bus, I was surprised to find Reagan and Jada waiting. I forgot we hung out with them the first time, but that was okay. I could still make this all work.

"What should we go on first?" Jada asked as we walked into the lobby. Her cinch bag was almost bigger than she was. "I want to go on that group tube ride. And that toilet bowl thing."

"Me too! The only big ride I got on last time was the Constrictor, but I haven't done the toilet bowl yet."

Jada looked at me strangely. "You've been here before?"

Oops. "No. I meant Taryn liked the Constrictor when she came." *Good save.*

"Reagan!" I saw her mom waving her down. She had a clipboard with names on it. Jada and Reagan headed over.

"This is going to be great, don't you think?" I said to Laura, getting excited now.

"Not if we're stuck in Reagan and Jada's group," she mumbled.

"What do you mean? We like hanging out with them." *Didn't we?*

"Yes, but . . ." Laura bit her lip. "Since we are doing this Jake thing, I don't think being in their group is the best idea."

"Why?" I asked, watching kids stream into the lobby.

"They don't talk about boys at all. They're not going to want to follow Jake around."

But today wasn't just about Jake. It was about us too. I

couldn't say that, though, so I just stood there and listened like a good best friend.

Laura pulled me into the gift shop in the lobby so no one could hear us. The two of us stood near the candy counter. "It's just that . . ." She eyed me hopefully. "I wasn't going to mention this, but Sarah and the other girls from the play have room for two more in their chaperone group. What if we switched?"

"I don't think we can do that," I said. Which was true.

"Maybe we can! And if we did, then we'd definitely bump into Jake because Ava is friends with him." She squealed. "What do you think? Can we switch? I wanted to ask you earlier, but my mom said to leave it alone."

So why aren't you? I wanted to say. I curled my toes into my flip-flops. If I answered wrong, it could get Laura upset. But if I said yes, we'd be spending all day with the drama queens. Laura looked so hopeful, I felt bad. "I guess, if you really want to be with them."

"Them and you!" Laura linked her arm through my free one. "This is great! I'll text Sarah. Reagan and Jada are nice, but you're going to really like Sarah and Ava! And Marisol is a whiz at memorizing lines. She taught me this method with flash cards, and it totally works. And Sarah does the best impressions. You should hear her mimic Tina Fey. We're going to have so much fun in their group."

But I wanted us to have fun without them. That was the whole point of coming back to this day and doing it over—to show Laura she didn't need their group when she already had me, and that I could help her get Jake too.

"Laura!" Steph walked into the gift shop with some of the others, and I froze. "Did you decide yet?"

Laura let go of my arm. "I'll be right back. Let me tell them."

I hovered around a stuffed-animal collection while Laura did the dirty work. I felt bad enough about ditching Jada and Reagan as it was. I turned the corner and spotted someone sitting on top of their backpack, reading *The Sea Stars* next to a stack of stuffed monkeys. "Clare?"

She looked up from her book, surprised. "Hey. Don't tell anyone you spotted me back here, okay? I'm trying to avoid the water park as long as I can."

I bet I knew why: Ava. "Why? Today is going to be fun! You should hang out with us."

Clare looked wistful. "I would, but I'm in Ava Sinclair's chaperone group, so . . ." She gulped hard and looked away. "I think I'm better off in here with my book."

I hated to think Clare spent the whole field trip hiding out in the gift shop. Suddenly, I felt torn. I wanted to help Clare, but I had to fix things with Laura first. I wasn't sure I could manage both in one retake. "Okay, but if you change your mind, I'm sure the groups will wind up on some rides together. Maybe we'll meet up on the lazy river."

She nodded, but still didn't look convinced. "Maybe."

"I love *The Sea Stars,* too, by the way," I added. It was a sci-fi adventure, which wasn't normally my thing, but the school librarian had recommended it, and I couldn't put it down.

"This is my third read," Clare said, perking up. "Are you Team Aaron or Team Amber?"

"Aaron, naturally," I said. "He's part mermaid. Hello."

"But Amber is a siren. Can't beat that either," Clare said. "Every time I read it, I find something else I love about the story. Did you know they're making it into a movie?"

"No, but now I want to read the book again," I said. "I keep trying to get it at the library, but it's always checked out."

Clare smiled. "When I finish this again—which will probably be today—you can borrow mine."

I grinned. "Okay."

"Zo-Zo!" Laura was waving me over to the candy counter.

"I have to go, but your hiding spot is safe with me," I told Clare.

"See you later. Maybe," Clare said, and went back to reading.

I weaved through the store around the candy counter and found Laura near the entrance.

"Guess what?" Laura asked.

"What?"

"We couldn't officially switch groups, but Ava had the

best idea to get around that—she told me to sign us in with our chaperone, so I did. And then we can sneak into the water park with Ava's group instead." She laughed nervously.

I paled. "Aren't we going to get in trouble?"

"Ava said it's not a big deal. No one will even notice we're gone. Ava said Jake and some of the boys are sneaking into the water park early after they've checked in with their chaperone so they can get on the rides first. We're going to follow them. But we have to hurry." Laura pulled me out of the gift shop and through the packed lobby.

Noooo. No matter what I did, the drama queens showed up and boys became an issue. How were we going to avoid Paradise Plunge now? When would we get our chance to reconnect? And how bad would Jada and Reagan feel when they learned we'd ditched them? This whole thing felt wrong. I stopped short. "I don't know about this."

Laura exhaled loudly. "Zoeeee." She sounded like Taryn. "Fine. If you don't want to go with us, don't. I'm going. I'll just catch up with you later."

Now Laura was ditching me too? I hesitated. If I didn't go with Laura, she'd think I wasn't cool, but if I went, we'd wind up in trouble. I couldn't let this whole retake be for nothing. Laura stared at me hopefully and I felt my resolve waffle. "No, I'll come," I said quickly. "You're right. No one will even notice we're gone, and this is the perfect chance for you to hang with Jake."

Laura cheered. "Yes! Ava didn't think you'd agree, but I knew she was wrong. Come on!" She grabbed my arm again. "This is going to be the best day. I can feel it!"

As I followed her through the lobby, I crossed my fingers and hoped Laura was right.

CHAPTER TWELVE

My heart was pumping wildly as Laura, the drama queens, and I slipped past the chaperones, who were going over rules, and snuck into the women's changing area to get into the water park unnoticed.

"Quick!" Hyacinth said as she burst through the exit into the half-empty park. "There are no lines!" Everyone started running.

I struggled to keep up. The park reminded me of being in a fishbowl—glass walls surrounding winding multicolored tubes and staircases. The place reeked of chlorine. In the middle was a huge wave pool and splash zone, and a giant three-story climber that had a huge bucket hanging above it. Every half hour a bell rang, and the bucket would dump all its water on the people waiting below.

Ava stopped short when we finally reached a ride called

Mountain Mayhem. For a moment I was actually excited. I never got to go on this ride the first time we were here.

"The boys are already on their way up," she said. "Let's catch them before they go on." She pulled off her cover-up, kicked off her flip-flops, tossed them onto a lounge chair, and ran up the stairs. The other girls followed.

"Come on, Zoe!" Laura told me, racing ahead of me.

I rushed to pull off my cover-up and follow the girls, taking the wet steps two at a time. By the last stair turn, my legs were burning.

"Great! We missed them!" Ava said as I reached the last step. I watched a redhead and a boy with black hair disappear on a tube into a tunnel. "Everyone back down. We need to see where they're going next."

"Can't we just go on the ride first?" I asked.

The lifeguard had a two-person tube just waiting for us.

"No way," Hyacinth said. "We don't want to ruin our hair before we see them. And besides, we haven't done a live video from the water park yet. I want my hair to look good for that."

"Or you could just put your hair up in a ponytail so it doesn't matter," suggested Marisol.

"Why didn't I think of that?" Steph sighed. "Then it wouldn't matter when we posted a video."

"Ooh, let's do a video of us screaming on a ride we're scared of," Sarah suggested.

"I'm not going on any of those rides with big drops," said Hyacinth. "Have you guys forgotten about Pukey Pete?"

Steph put her arm around her. "Stop worrying! We'd never make you go on anything alone. You're my ride or die!" Hyacinth put her head on Steph's shoulder, and I looked at them in surprise. The drama queens were much nicer to one another than I'd realized.

I looked from the waiting tube to Laura. "How about you? Want to ride down and meet them at the bottom? I could care less what my hair looks like."

I could already picture the two of us screaming with laughter as the tube took the first bumpy turn. We needed a bonding moment!

Laura bit her lip and looked from me to the others already heading down the stairs. "I don't know. If Ava is going to post a video of all of us . . ."

"Beach hair, don't care." That had always been our motto. "Or in this case, water park hair."

"Yeah, but I haven't seen Jake yet. I think I'll just walk back down," Laura said. "Are you mad?"

"No," I said, even though I was disappointed. But I wasn't going to tell her that.

"You go!" Laura suggested. "And I'll meet you at the bottom."

I thought again about Taryn's text—I needed to learn to do what I wanted sometimes too. I turned to the lifeguard. "Can I ride this one alone?"

146

He shook his head. "Sorry. I only have two-person tubes left right now."

Well, that answered that question. Laura was gone by the time I turned around. I reached the bottom and followed them up the stairs to the Storm Chaser, but by the time we got up there, the boys were already riding.

"Forget it, let's just go on the ride. I'm tired of waiting," Steph suggested, and I was relieved. I wanted to get on a ride already. "Wait! First, everyone squeeze in for a selfie." She held up a phone in a waterproof case. "Say 'Aquatopia'!"

I got sandwiched in the middle as the others crowded around, and I looked wildly for Laura. She was in this shot at least. The lifeguard and everyone on the growing line didn't look thrilled we were holding up the queue.

"Aquatopia!" everyone yelled, and Steph took the picture.

We inched up in line and finally reached the front.

"Where are your tubes?" the lifeguard asked. "Didn't you carry them up?"

We all looked at one another and then at the people on line behind us, who were now pushing past us. They all had two-person tubes. I couldn't believe we had to get off again!

Sarah groaned. "I can't believe we have to walk down."

"This time we wait at the bottom of the ride for the guys," Marisol suggested, sounding annoyed. "When we run into them, we'll suggest we all go on a ride together."

The others nodded in agreement and headed down the stairs again. This was exhausting. I touched Laura's arm. "I say we wave the white flag and find Jake later. Let's go on something already! I feel like we've spent the last hour going up and down stairs and getting nowhere. I'm hot, tired, and my thighs are literally sticking together it's so steamy," I joked.

Laura looked torn. "I know, but we're so close to getting on a ride with Jake! The others don't know I like him yet, so I need you there with me. Please? Can we keep trying? Don't you want to hang out with the guys?"

I just want to go on a ride with my best friend. But that's not the answer Laura wanted to hear. She was so into Jake she couldn't concentrate on anything else. It didn't help that the drama queens were obsessed with Jake's friends. Even on line, when we weren't with them, they were watching the boys' live videos from the park. Didn't they want to enjoy Aquatopia?

I know I did. I was hoping this retake would give me a chance to spend the day with my best friend, but it was clear that wasn't going to happen till she got Jake face time first.

"Of course," I lied.

Laura smiled and headed down the stairs while I tried not to look as defeated as I felt. At least Ava had been right about waiting for the boys in the splash zone of the Constrictor. When Shardul, Dougie, Jake, and a few other boys emerged from the tubes into the splash zone, we were already waiting.

"Who came in first?" Dougie asked as he waded out of the splashdown pool, his black hair dripping. "I didn't see—Shardul or Jake?" Sarah was busy staring at Shardul's taut, tan stomach.

"Shardul," Ava said at the same time Laura called out "Jake." They both sort of laughed.

Shardul shook his head. "I totally won. They're just covering for you, Jakey boy. Someone here must like you!" The other boys whistled, and Laura's face grew red-hot. Ava didn't even flinch.

"What are you going on next, Shardul?" Sarah asked as she played with a hair tie wrapped around her wrist.

"Not sure. What haven't we gone on, Dougie?" Shardul asked him as he shook out his dark hair.

Dougie was busy jumping in and out of a tube on the floor. "The Venus Slydetrap!" He looked up and grinned. "Seats up to six, ladies. Any takers?"

"Maybe," Ava said as I heard Marisol audibly inhale. "You going on now?"

"Now," Jake insisted. "Let's go." He headed to the ride's line, and the other girls followed. Laura grinned and rushed to the front of the group to walk near him.

I heard my phone buzz, and I took it out of the waterproof pouch I was carrying it in to read the text.

Mom: Where are u????? Reagan's mom said you ditched your group. I tracked you so I know you're in the water park, but text me you're okay! Make sure Laura checks in too. Dianne said Laura isn't answering texts. This isn't like you.

Even in this new reality, I was letting my mom down. What was I doing here? Clare was sitting on the floor of the gift shop alone. Laura and I weren't getting any time together, and I still wasn't getting on rides. I quickly texted Mom to apologize as I climbed the next set of stairs. When I reached the top, the boys were talking to one another, and the girls were standing around watching them. I went over to Laura.

"My mom texted," I told her. "Your mom and my mom are mad we ditched our group."

"Ignore the text," Ava butted in. "That's what I did when my mom asked where Clare Stelton was." She rolled her eyes. "Like I would ever hang out with her." Hyacinth giggled.

I felt my skin prickle. *She used to be your best friend,* I wanted to shout. "Why? Clare is so nice." Everyone looked at me, including Ava.

"Yeah, but she's into robotics," Ava said, as if that were a bad thing. And I guess it was to Laura, too, who started twirling her hair around her finger, like she did when she was nervous. I could tell she was thinking about Future City. Maybe she thought I was going to tell Ava we were in the club. But all I cared about was sticking up for Clare.

"I feel like every school has a robotics club now because it's so popular. Weren't you in a robotics club with her in elementary school? I thought I heard your group won a robotics contest," I said casually, and the other girls looked at her.

Ava pushed a strand of hair behind her right ear. "Let's just go on the ride already. We're coming with you guys!" she shouted to Jake as he, Dougie, and Shardul climbed into a tube.

The next moment happened so fast I didn't have time to react. Ava took Laura's arm and Laura grabbed my arm and we headed toward the boys' tube, grabbing the last three spots.

"Hey!" Hyacinth shouted, but the raft was full. I crammed my legs between the tangle of feet just in time for the raft to push off. I looked back at the other girls as we drifted into the tunnel and disappeared.

"Don't anyone puke!" Dougie said, laughing hysterically as he twisted his hands to fit inside the rope holds, giving me no room to hold on. Laura was still gripping my right arm since she was sandwiched between me and Jake.

"Yeah, there's no Pukey Petes in this raft, is there?" Shardul asked as he stretched out his brown legs, banging into ours as we hit the first bend in the tube. Everyone screamed.

I glanced at Laura. She tended to get carsick. Her mom always drove with the air-conditioning blasted on long rides and had Laura sip something with bubbles to calm her stomach. This ride might not have been the best move for her.

"What's this big drop like again?" Jake asked as we bumped along.

"Dude, it's the toilet-bowl one!" Dougie said as water splashed into the side of the tube, soaking Ava's hair. "Spins us, then drops us like we've been flushed."

"Flushed! Epic!" Shardul said.

Laura shut her eyes tight as we rounded another bend and then fell into nothingness. We all screamed as the giant raft shot down a ravine into a vortex of water. The raft went down one side and shot back up the other side.

"How are we not flipping?" Ava yelled as the boys roared with laughter.

"We're going to flip! We're going to flip!" Laura cried.

But we didn't. I held on tight as the raft drifted into the next tube and we shot along till we landed in a giant wave pool, water washing over the entire raft.

"That. Was. Awesome!" Jake pointed to Laura. "You totally freaked out."

Laura no longer looked terrified. Now she was smiling. "Me? You should have heard you scream!"

"I did not scream," Jake said, and the two of them spent the next few minutes debating who screamed louder.

Seeing them, I felt relieved. Laura was talking to Jake and was happy. Mission accomplished. Now we could move on to the Laura-and-Zoe portion of the day.

What did I suggest we do next? A slide with mats? A two-person tube ride? We needed bonding time, and there was so much I wanted us to go on together. My thoughts were interrupted by the screams of the other drama queens as their tube shot out of the tunnel and landed in the pool next to us.

"That was so much fun!" Hyacinth shouted as she waded out to join us. "I was scared but not scared, and then—"

"The tube dropped and Marisol got all this water in her mouth," Steph finished as she pulled her hair into a ponytail with one of her teal hair ties.

I watched Laura pull a hair tie off her wrist and do the same thing. The band was teal, just like the other girls'. When I looked around, I realized all of them had teal hair ties. Even back then, she was becoming part of their group. How had I not noticed it before?

The park was filling up now. I could see Fairview kids running for the wave pool and others headed to the lazy river behind us. Our strange new group was just standing in the splash zone, talking about the ride we'd just gone on. I was itching for someone to move on and head to a new ride, but I didn't want to interrupt Laura's conversation with Jake.

"Zo-Zo!" Laura suddenly said, and I looked up. "Come on! We're going again!" She and the other girls were already following Jake, Shardul, and Dougie back on line.

"Zo-Zo, come on!" I heard Dougie mimic.

I could handle one more run with the group, but then Laura and I were definitely going off on our own.

Or not.

We ended up going on the ride two more times. Then we went on two rides on two-person tubes, one of which Laura got to go on with Jake after Dougie practically insisted they go together. I was happy for Laura, but now she barely noticed I was there. She barely noticed I was there. Every time I suggested we ditch the group, Laura found an excuse to stay with everyone.

I really thought doing a retake of Aquatopia would bring us closer, but I'd never felt further away.

"Lazy river next!" Dougie shouted, and the group ran to the line. Somehow, I wound up at the back of the pack. By the time I reached the front, Laura and Jake were already floating away, with Ava and Sarah behind them. Shardul and the other boys dove in and out of their tubes. The rest of the girls were paddling fast, trying to catch up.

"Stay in your tube!" I heard a lifeguard shout, but the group was already turning a bend. No one even noticed I was missing.

"Zoe?"

I turned around. Reagan, Jada, and Clare were on line behind me. I let a ton of people cut me so I could reach them. The three of them were wet from head to toe, but smiling.

"Where have you been?" Reagan asked. "We've been looking everywhere for you. My mom was worried."

"I'm so sorry," I apologized, my face reddening. "Laura ran off and I followed, and . . . I'm just sorry. I'll go find your mom and explain." Maybe it was better I got back to the present anyway, before anything got screwed up again.

"Don't be silly!" she said. "I'll just text her that we found you. That way you can go on the lazy river with us." She whipped out her phone and did it before I could even argue. "She got a cabana with the other chaperones—I think it's called Castaway B—so she's there if we need her."

I couldn't believe Reagan was being so good about this. Laura would have freaked out if I ran off on her like that.

Jada looked around. "Hey. Where is Laura?"

"She's on the lazy river with Jake Graser and some people from the play," I said, and they all nodded knowingly.

"You can hang with us, then," said Jada. "We found Clare here hanging in the gift shop and convinced her to go on rides with us."

I was happy to see Clare in the water park and glad the others weren't mad at me. It couldn't hurt to go on a few more rides before I left. Laura was having a good time, and like Taryn said, I deserved to have fun too. "I'd love to hang with you guys."

"Then let's go on some real rides!" Clare's eyes brightened. "We can float on the lazy river anytime."

We all looked at one another. Then we ditched the line and ran.

CHAPTER THIRTEEN

Being with Reagan, Jada, and Clare was a lot different from following the drama queens. The girls didn't care about their hair being a mess, trailing the boys on rides, having matching hair ties, or doing live videos from the water park. No one even pulled their phones out of their waterproof pouches. We were just having fun together sailing along in a tube at top speed. We rode the toilet bowl three times, did a body slide, and rode a two-person slide, each grabbing a partner with zero drama. No one cared about seeing Jake Graser or even going on Paradise Plunge. I'd spent a lot of time with Reagan and Jada at Future City, but I'd never hung out with Clare before, and she was funny—*really* funny. She seemed to open up more as the day went on. I was having such a good time, I almost forgot all about the Retake app or Laura.

"I think it's time." Clare grinned and looked at us. "Should we tackle FlowRider?"

"FlowRider!" we all shouted, and ran out of the wave pool we'd been bobbing in.

The FlowRider surf simulator was the attraction everyone talked about and rarely attempted. Forget Paradise Plunge—this ride was the real water park test. And if you failed, everyone would see it. The surf simulator sat at the entrance to the park and had a huge viewing area where crowds gathered to watch. It looked like a skateboard ramp with a waterfall that riders would attempt to surf on a controlled wave. We watched people go a few times before we got on line. Riders went in groups of two, started out lying down, and then attempted to stand up on their boards and ride the wave. Most seemed to go flying off, which was when the crowd cheered the most. Despite how hard surfing looked, the ride had the longest line.

"Are you nervous?" Jada asked as we inched forward. "I'm nervous."

"Nah." Reagan had her eye on the wave. "Who cares if you fall?"

"That girl got up." Clare pointed to someone in the simulator. "See how she stayed low on the board for a while before she got on her knees? I think that's the trick. We've got this."

Jada frowned. "Maybe I'll just bodyboard."

"No! We have to try to stand up!" Clare insisted. "Who cares if people laugh? I'm so tired of worrying what people think of me all the time." She sighed. "I'm going to try."

"Me too," Reagan decided.

"So will I," I said, and we all looked at Jada, who smiled. "Okay, why not? Let's do it."

Clare was so supportive. I really liked that about her. The drama queens seemed to support one another, too, but there was still that competitiveness. With these girls, my stomach wasn't in knots, and I wasn't worrying about every word coming out of my mouth. It was a nice change.

Before I knew it, it was our turn to ride. Reagan and Jada went first. Reagan tumbled off right away, but she was laughing. Jada hit the wave while on her stomach, and we watched as she slowly got to her knees and stayed there the whole ride, which was more than she thought she could do.

"Woo-hoo!" Clare and I cheered, doing a goofy victory dance on line.

Clare and I were up next. She headed to the left side and I went to the right, each of us grabbing a large white surfboard from the lifeguard. My chest was pounding.

"You'll have to leave your phone on the side," the lifeguard said when he saw it around my neck.

"But . . ." Nothing could happen to this phone. *Nothing.*

"I'll wear it," the lifeguard offered, as if he could hear my thoughts. "It will be fine."

I handed it over and watched anxiously as he placed it around his neck.

"Go, Zoe!" I heard someone shout, and assumed it was Reagan and Jada, but I didn't look. Instead, I concentrated on the lifeguard's instructions and got ready to drop my board into position when they turned the simulator on. It was kind of exciting. I looked over at Clare, who was about to do the same. She gave me a thumbs-up, and then the buzzer sounded, water started gushing, and the lifeguard shouted, "Go!"

I took a deep breath and dropped. The mist from the board hitting the wave made it hard to see, but I held tight, trying to find my balance. The wave was making the board bounce up and down and sway side to side across the simulator, but I tried to remember what I'd seen other riders do before me. Slowly, I pulled my knees up to my chest, trying to curl them under me. *I will not fall,* I told myself. *I will not fall!* Next I tried to sit up on my knees. That was so hard that it seemed smarter to skip that part and just attempt to stand. I stared straight ahead like I was on a balance beam (wasn't that what they always told us to do in gym?) and pulled myself up to standing. *Yes!*

I could hear screaming and cheers over the sound of the rushing water, but the loudest sound was the whooshing in my ears. I started to count how long I was up there. . . . Five seconds . . . ten . . . fifteen . . . twenty. I heard the buzzer sound, and the simulator slowly started to shut off, the board coasting off the wave into the pool with me on it. I skidded onto the mat at the same time Clare did.

"I did it!" she said, laughing.

"Me too!" We high-fived.

A crowd was gathered in front of the simulator. Jada and Reagan were in the front, screaming and jumping up and down. I wiped the water out of my eyes, exited the pool, and came face to face with Laura's crew.

"Look at you, Surf God!" Dougie shouted as Shardul and Jake high-fived me.

"That was amazing!" said Hyacinth, who was standing with Marisol and Stephanie. "I was afraid to get up there and fall in front of everyone so I didn't do it."

I didn't think the drama queens were afraid of anything. "Clare said we should just go for it so we did." I smiled at her. "It was really fun."

"We know. The rest of us tried it and fell," Shardul admitted. "But at least we didn't wipe out like Laura."

Dougie shuddered. "There was blood and everything."

My heart stopped. "Did you say Laura?"

Jake made a face. "Yeah, she crashed into the side of the simulator and cut her knee bad. They took her to first aid."

"I should go check on her," I told Clare.

"Tell her we hope she feels better," Clare said.

I quickly followed the signs to first aid and found Laura sitting on a table with her knee bandaged. She was holding an ice pack that was dripping as if it had already melted. She and Sarah were talking to the lifeguard. Laura saw me and looked away. Sarah gave me a small nod.

"You're free to go, but I'd avoid going back in the water with an open wound," the lifeguard was saying.

"Thanks," Laura said, but I could tell from her voice she was upset.

"I'm going to get you some more ice packs to take with you. You can crack it and put it on your knee later." When the lifeguard walked into another room, I ran over to Laura.

"Are you okay?" I asked.

"No. I fell," Laura said flatly.

"She was on the surf rider, and her knee hit the wall," Sarah explained.

"I heard," I told them, "and came right here. At least you didn't break anything," I said optimistically.

"Yeah, but I embarrassed myself in front of Jake and half the sixth grade!" Laura's eyes filled with tears. "I practically rolled off the simulator! Dougie was videoing. It's probably online by now! I'm going to be the new Pukey Pete." She put her head in her hands.

"He wouldn't do that," I insisted, but Sarah gave me a look behind Laura's back that told me the video was probably already viral. "Even if he did, you didn't puke on a ride. You fell. Most people do. It was really hard to stay up on the simulator."

Laura looked up. "You went on it without me?"

I blinked. "Yeah. But so did you."

Laura covered her face and mumbled through her fingertips. "Jake didn't even come with me to first aid. Sarah was the only one sweet enough to walk me over since you were nowhere to be found." She glared at me. "What happened to you? We were on the lazy river and you just disappeared."

"You were gone before I even got a tube," I pointed out. "You were with Jake and the other"—I stopped myself from saying "drama queens"—"girls."

"When I turned around, you were just gone, and Hyacinth said you went off with Reagan and Jada," Laura said accusingly. "You didn't even tell any of us you were going."

"Because you were already gone," I said again. "I was the one who wanted us to go on rides together today, remember?"

"We were on rides together!" Laura said.

She wasn't getting it. I wanted today to be a chance for us to have fun together. I really thought she'd go on one ride with Jake, and then we'd go off alone. But I was starting to realize our friendship wasn't enough anymore—for Laura or for me. It wasn't wrong, but it didn't feel great being replaced.

"Jake probably thinks I'm an idiot," Laura said, and

Sarah nodded sympathetically. "If you were there, I wouldn't have gone on the simulator."

I gaped. "How is this my fault?"

Laura shrugged. "You should just go. Sarah said she'd sit with me in the cabana till we head back to the bus to go home. I'm sure Reagan and Jada are waiting for you."

That was a dig if I ever heard one. So, she was allowed to have new friends, but I wasn't? I wanted to scream. The Retake app let me redo this moment, but nothing had changed.

I didn't understand. Why wasn't this retake working either? I had to think of a different moment I could go back to. Maybe if I scrolled through my feed again . . . *My phone!* I'd left it with the lifeguard. "I have to go," I mumbled, and took off.

I ran all the way back to the wave simulator, cutting the line to get to the top. When I spotted the lifeguard wearing my phone around his neck, I silently cheered.

"Hey!" Hyacinth said when she saw me. She was at the front of the line with the other girls and Jake, Shardul, and Dougie. "How is Laura?"

"She can't go on any more water rides," I told them, "so she's upset. She's headed to the cabana. She'd probably love to see you guys." I looked at Jake.

"We'll try to go by," Jake said, answering for everyone. "We want to get on this ride again first."

At least it wasn't a straight-up no. If Jake showed up in

the cabana, Laura couldn't stay mad at me. But would he still go if I left? This app made everything so complicated. I had to hope he would.

"Go on again with us," Hyacinth said. The buzzer sounded and a new set of riders got into position. "I want to see how you do this."

"I should really get back to Laura." There was no way I was staying here and messing up things even more. "I just came back to grab my phone. See you later!" I flagged down the lifeguard.

"Was wondering when you'd be back." He lifted the phone off his neck and handed it to me. "You better take that phone out of the pouch. It's overheating."

"Thanks!" I immediately opened the seal. The phone was really hot now. What if it completely shut down? I tapped the screen. The phone was still working, but this wasn't good. If the app fried my phone, I could get stuck in the past. Even if that didn't happen, I could still wind up with a broken phone that my parents would never replace. I needed to make sure this next retake worked, in case I didn't get another shot at this. But shouldn't I at least get back to the present first, to see what was going on? If Jake went to check on Laura, she'd probably forgive me. For all I knew, things could be fine with us in the present. I took a deep breath.

Okay, that was the plan: Check out the present, and if

things were bad, I'd hopefully have one more chance at a retake before my phone fried.

I just needed to find somewhere private to travel back to the present, because I still had no clue how this Retake app worked. What if I just disappeared in front of a crowd? Seeing signs for the changing rooms, I headed there, searching for an empty row of lockers. When I found one, I opened the app, my fingers practically burning at the touch of the phone.

The picture of us from this morning was already loaded into the app. It said #aquatopiaboundbffs, and Laura and I were both tagged in it. The picture was glowing, rather than faded, which was different from what had happened at the sleepover. Maybe that was a sign that Laura and I were okay. I scrolled forward, passing pictures from June—this time Laura was in all of them—and searched for a photo in the present.

"*Mom!* Which locker number are we?"

"It's 742!" a mom yelled back.

I looked at the locker numbers in front of me. They were in the 730s.

People were coming. I had to be fast. I scrolled as far forward as I could go, landing on a new picture of Laura and me from September 6—the first day of school. I didn't even read the hashtag or see where we were. We were together on the first day of seventh grade. That's all that mattered. I clicked on the button and closed my eyes. "Please send me back to the first day of seventh grade."

"Zoe?"

I opened my eyes. Clare was standing in the locker row, looking surprised.

There was a blinding flash, and I was gone.

CHAPTER FOURTEEN

"Say 'First day of seventh grade'!" Dad shouted, and then I was greeted by another flash, courtesy of Dad's camera.

"First day of seventh grade!" Laura shouted.

She was standing beside me, her hair tied up in a messy bun, and she was wearing a pink paisley shift dress that looked like one of those expensive designer ones we were always looking at longingly. I looked down—we were not matching. I was wearing a teal graphic tee that said "Sunscreen, Sun, Sand, Repeat" and jeans (not white ones!).

I breathed a sigh of relief. Things had to be good between us if we were going to the first day of seventh grade together! Jake must have shown up at the cabana to check on Laura, told her I sent him, and everything between us was good again. Maybe I didn't even need another retake!

I could just delete this app off my phone so it stopped running hot, and stay right where I was in the present.

"Hey." Laura nudged me. "Why are you zoning out?"

"I'm not zoning out," I insisted.

She laughed. "Yes, you are! Who are you thinking about?" she whispered in my ear. "Dougie?"

I stepped back. "I am *not* thinking about Dougie."

Her phone buzzed. "It's my dad," she said, surprised. "I guess he's calling since he isn't here for the first day. I'll just take this over there." She pointed to the driveway, and I nodded.

I waited till Laura slipped away to pull out my phone. It was practically burning through my jeans pocket and it was only charged to 45 percent now. I flipped through the apps till I found Retake. My finger hovered over the app. I should delete it now, before it destroyed my phone. But . . . what if things weren't as perfect as they seemed?

"Zoe!" Taryn came flying out the front door with wet hair and charged toward me.

"Hey!" I said, happy to see her.

Taryn gave me a look. "Don't 'hey' me."

Uh-oh.

"I am not covering for you with Mom and Dad," Taryn hissed. "If you're going to ride your bike all the way to the Eaton movie theater after school today, then you deserve to be caught."

"Eaton?" I wasn't even allowed to ride my bike up to the

pizza place because Mom thought it was too far from the house. And I had to check in every hour no matter where I was in town. Laura and I basically rode to each other's houses or to one of the coffee spots in town, and they were all within a few blocks of one another. Why would I ever ride to Eaton?

"Don't play dumb. Avery saw you last night when she was on her way to Chili's with her mom. That's two towns away on your bike, crossing over Marywood Turnpike. What were you thinking? A kid on a bike got hit there last week!"

"Sorry, Mom," I joked, but Taryn didn't laugh.

"You keep saying you want my advice about everything, including what's been going on with you and Laura, but you never take it." Taryn actually sounded hurt. "I tell you to do one thing, and you do the exact opposite. I don't know why I bother. I told you all she cared about was hanging out with that kid Josh."

My heart pounded as I tried to get up to speed. "Do you mean Jake? Or is there a Josh now too? What's going on with me and Laura?"

"Zoe! Marisol's mom is here!" Dad called. "Laura is already in the car!"

Marisol's . . . ? That meant . . .

Dad handed me a lunch bag. "Here. Mom and I talked. You can't buy every day. I don't care what Laura is allowed to do."

I never wanted to buy again after what happened the first time. "Dad . . . ," I started to say.

"We'll talk after school," Dad said gently. "And your mom said to try to work on Laura, okay? Dianne is really worried about her. First you two quit Future City, and now you don't want to try out for volleyball." He hesitated. "Just promise me you won't give up everything you love just because Laura doesn't want to do it."

"I won't," I insisted. But had I already done that in this new present? "I'll even send you a picture of me at volleyball tryouts today."

Dad laughed. "You don't have to go that far. But maybe we could stick with our traditional first-night-of-school dinner tonight?" Both Dad and Taryn looked at me hopefully. If she wanted to go for hibachi, we had to be in a good place.

"I'd like that." I gave Taryn a hug and ran to Marisol's mom's massive SUV. I opened the door and jumped into the third row with Steph and Ava, who were singing along to something on the radio at the top of their lungs. Laura was already in the second row, scrolling on her phone and singing half-heartedly along with them. I heard her sigh heavily as we pulled out of the driveway.

She turned around and looked at us. "My mom is driving me insane! She said I can't go out tonight."

"Go out? Don't we have dinner tonight at Izumi?" I asked.

Laura made a face. "Yeah, but we told our moms no, remember? You did tell your mom no, didn't you?"

"Yeah," I said quickly. Had I screwed things up already? "But my dad is still pushing for it."

"Tell him we're doing something with our friends," Laura said pointedly. "Why are they being so annoying about this? Ava's having us over tonight."

"Yeah," Ava said, and looked at me. "And everyone is invited, unlike your family dinner thing that's just your two families."

Laura rolled her eyes. "I know, it's so silly. My mom was going on like 'This is family time! It's not going to be summer all over again. You can't hang out with your friends every day. She almost didn't let me come to breakfast this morning because she says all I do is ask for money.'"

I heard a beep. My phone charge had dropped to 35 percent. I really should have grabbed a charger. The way this conversation was going, I was starting to think I still needed the Retake. But what if the phone died beforehand? Would the app just disappear?

"Uh, Mrs. Tolman? Can I use your phone charger?" I asked awkwardly.

"Mine is broken, sweetie, sorry!" Mrs. Tollman pulled over in front of the bagel store. "All right, girls. Enjoy breakfast. Just watch the time. Are you sure you don't want me to wait and drive you to school after?"

172

"Mom, we're fine," Marisol said huffily as she exited the car first. "We can walk two blocks." The rest of us filed out after her.

"'Boys, boys, boys, that's all you talk about!'" Laura said, still talking about her mom. "'You need to focus on school more than YouTube videos of makeup!'"

I just nodded. There were so many gaps in our story that I wasn't sure what was real and what wasn't. In the past I knew every place we'd been before—the great days, the bad ones, along with the things we'd stayed up late talking about and wishing for. But now with Retake, there were these missing chunks of time taking us from one moment and shooting us into a new one. As great as it was to retake moments, I didn't know the Laura I was coming back to. And that was really scary.

"Why doesn't she see I'm older now?" Laura asked. "I want to hang out with my friends, not our parents."

I winced. I always liked our first-day-of-school tradition.

"Things change," Laura added.

"Things change." I guess that was what I was most afraid of. I followed Laura into the stream of cool air-conditioning blasting out of the bagel store. The other girls walked ahead of us, not waiting. I tried to play peacemaker. "Couldn't we do dinner and then go to Ava's?"

"Zoe." Laura sighed as she opened her bag and pulled out a lip gloss. She applied it looking in the mirrored side of the drinks fridge. "Don't be weird about this again."

"Weird about what?" I really didn't know what she was talking about.

Laura finished with her lip gloss and turned to me. "Hanging out with the guys. Your mom doesn't have to know. And you don't have to like anyone there to go. I'm not telling my mom."

"You're not?" My mom would freak if she heard I was hanging out at a boy's house without permission, even if we were just friends.

"No, and you can't tell your mom either." Laura gave me the stink eye. "Because your mom will tell my mom, and then we'll both be toast." She looked at me pleadingly. "I really want to see Jake, so don't screw it up like last time."

How had I screwed things up last time? "I'm not. I didn't realize you and Jake were a thing."

Laura blushed. "Kind of. Maybe? I mean, ever since that day at Aquatopia, we've been texting. And he talked to me when we were at the cabana this summer, but then he was gone most of August because his family has a place in the Poconos. I don't know." She curled a strand of hair around her finger with its manicured pink nail. "Dougie says he hasn't said anything, and even though Ava is with Shardul now, he barely talks to her at all, let alone talks about me and Jake. Maybe Hyacinth can find out from Peter, or Marisol can talk to Connor. They might know something. I have to ask them."

"Does everyone have a boyfriend?" I asked, surprised.

Laura checked her lip gloss in the reflection of the mirrored countertop full of pastries. "You're the only who doesn't, but guess what? Ava says Max likes you! We can forget about setting you up with Dougie."

"Max who?" I asked.

"Max Tanner. Jake's friend? The one on the Sharks with him? He's going to Dougie's house tonight too—you know we're not actually going to Ava's, right? We just told the moms that. So if you go, then maybe you and Max can talk, and then we'd all have boyfriends." She grinned.

But I didn't know who Max was! How did I know I even wanted him to be my boyfriend? Did I have to have a boyfriend to hang out with Laura and the drama queens? I hadn't had much experience with boys yet. They seemed to speak a totally different language, and so many of them just burped or farted and laughed about it like it was cool. I couldn't even understand best friend code anymore. How would I speak boy?

"Maybe," I said, since Laura was still looking at me expectantly.

"Come on!" Laura got huffy. "You need to be with someone, too, or . . ." She trailed off. "You just do, okay? Come to Dougie's. Just don't be all weird."

There was that word again. What did Laura mean by that?

"Laura! Zoe!" Hyacinth was waving us over to a table. Everyone was squished into a corner booth, tie-dyed bagels in front of them along with drinks. They were laughing hysterically.

Sarah high-fived Ava. "That was epic! She totally thought you were inviting her to sit with us!"

"Did you see her face?" Ava asked. "I was just trying to tell her she had toilet paper on her shoe. She's so sensitive!"

"Who?" Laura asked, sitting down.

Ava shook her head. "Forget it. It's so not important."

"We got you a bagel," Sarah told Laura. She looked at me. "The line is short, Zoe, if you want one too." I heard one of the girls snort. Laura looked away awkwardly.

The drama queens and I had obviously cooled off since my last retake.

"Zoe, you aren't wearing pink," Hyacinth pointed out.

"Oh. I forgot." I noticed them look at one another. Laura pretended to be busy unwrapping her bagel. She was wearing pink. Why hadn't she reminded me this morning before we left?

Laura picked up her bagel. "The blue-and-green tie-dyed bagels are back! I love them!"

"Me too," said Sarah. "Remember when we took that picture of us balancing a stack of them on our heads?" The two of them started to giggle.

I didn't have a picture of that on the Retake app, so clearly I hadn't been there for that moment.

"Let's do it again now," Laura suggested.

"No, gross!" Ava said. "Let's just take a picture of us with our bagels." She held up her phone and the bagel for a selfie. "Everyone crowd in."

I didn't have a bagel, but Laura pulled me in close anyway.

"Smile!" Ava said as she snapped the picture. She quickly sent it to all our phones, and I heard mine ping.

I looked around. Every girl was quickly posting the photo to their social media. I got a flurry of alerts almost immediately. The alerts were going to eat up my phone power.

"I should go get a bagel," I told Laura. "I'll be right back." What were the chances I'd find a phone charger for sale in a bagel store? Slim to none, and I really needed my phone to work if I wanted another retake. This wasn't good.

Marisol didn't look up. "What are we hashtagging this shot?"

"Bagel bosses?" suggested Steph.

"I like that," agreed Ava.

I left them to their hashtags. As I got on the superlong line, my phone was making strange noises. When I pulled it out of my pocket, I noticed the power was down to 22 percent! Even worse, there was now an ominous message on the screen.

Do you want to go into power-saver mode? Some apps will be unavailable during this time.

No! What if one of those apps that became unavailable was Retake? Or my phone actually died, and the app died along with it? I couldn't believe I'd thought this morning that I could just delete the app. Laura and I were talking, yes, but she was acting weird, which meant things weren't great between us. But were they bad enough that I needed another retake? I had to admit, time travel was getting exhausting.

"The register is down, so it will be a few minutes, folks!" the guy behind the counter yelled to everyone on line.

I didn't have a few minutes. I had to find a charger. Maybe there was a store nearby that sold one. I headed back to the table to tell the others where I was going and got stuck one table away behind a mom trying to put a squirmy toddler into his stroller.

"You think she'll tell on you?" I heard someone say. "Don't invite her, then."

"She's not going to even talk to any of the guys. She'll just stand there looking awkward."

I froze. Were they talking about me?

"She'll probably have to leave early to go to Future City anyway." That voice sounded like Ava's.

"Definitely. I told her I was quitting, but she was like 'I like the club and I'm staying.'" That voice was my supposed best friend's.

My cheeks burned.

"Why are you guys still friends? You're so different!"

"I don't know. We've been friends forever. But lately she's

been acting so odd about us hanging out with the guys," I heard Laura say. "She doesn't even like any of them, so what is she even doing there? She's obsessed with knowing who's dating who. She just asked me about it again."

That's because I don't know what is happening in this reality! I wanted to shout.

"Maybe she's jealous," Sarah suggested.

"Zoe isn't like that," Laura said. "I think. She's just such a baby."

Was that what my best friend really thought of me? That because she was wearing makeup and hanging out with boys, she was cooler than I was? Forget about telling them where I was going. I was already gone. I turned around fast and banged into two construction workers headed to a table.

"Sorry, kid!" one said loudly.

Laura looked over and instantly knew I'd heard them. Her face crumbled as she stood up.

But for once, I didn't want to hear what Laura had to say. I ducked around a mom taking bagel orders from four kids and maneuvered past the long line at the counter. The exit was blocked, so I changed directions and searched for a bathroom. I refused to cry in front of everyone at Bagel Boss. When I turned the corner and saw the sign for a unisex restroom, I ran in and locked the door behind me.

"This is occupied!" someone said in a strangled voice.

"Sorry!" I turned and saw a girl with pink hair crying.

"Clare?"

She was sitting under the window, on one of half a dozen boxes of toilet paper. The walls were so thin I could hear people calling out breakfast sandwich orders in the kitchen.

"Are you okay? I didn't know anyone was in here," I explained. "It wasn't locked."

"It's okay. It's my fault." Clare wiped her eyes and stood up. She was wearing a "Skip the Straw! Save the Sea Turtles!" tee that matched her huge gray hoop earrings. "I darted in here so fast to get away, I didn't lock the door."

Now the conversation I overheard Ava having at the table when we arrived was starting to make sense. She must have been talking about Clare. "Is everything okay?" I asked.

"It's fine." Clare took a deep breath. "Actually, it's not fine. I don't know. Maybe I overreacted. I swore I wouldn't let her get to me again this year." She ran a hand through her hair. "Sorry. I know I'm not making sense."

"It's okay," I said gently. "Do you want to talk about it?"

She exhaled slowly. "There's not a lot to talk about. My best friend doesn't want to be friends anymore. She's got a new group, and she doesn't want me to be a part of it."

I knew this story too well. "I'm sorry."

"Me too. I don't get what happened between us, but I have to stop caring." Clare wiped her eyes again as the tears started coming. "It just hurts too much. I hate change."

"I do too," I admitted.

Everything was changing, and I couldn't stand it. Even in this new reality, Laura didn't find me cool enough anymore. Why did things have to change? My eyes started filling with tears.

"Oh no! Now I've made you cry!" Clare said.

"I'm fine!" I said, and we both started laughing through the tears.

The whole situation was kind of absurd—Clare and I were hiding in the Bagel Boss bathroom, crying over the same group of mean girls. There was a part of me that just wanted to turn to Clare and say *Let's get out of here.* But I didn't know this new reality any better than I knew the last one.

I just wanted to go home.

"Okay, enough!" Clare said suddenly. "We are not starting seventh grade like this."

"We're not!" I agreed.

"No more crying." Clare handed me a piece of toilet paper to wipe my eyes and dabbed her own as well.

"No more crying." I blotted my eyes.

"And no more crying in bathrooms," she added, starting to smile.

"No more crying in bathrooms," I seconded.

And that's when I realized Clare was a glass-half-full girl, like I usually was. It was the retakes that were making me second-guess everything.

"I don't know how sixth grade was for you, but I am *not* spending seventh grade hiding in a bathroom," Clare added.

My stomach twisted when I heard her say that. No one should have to hide in a bathroom all the time, even if that was what we both were currently doing.

"Sorry." Clare blushed. "I know you don't know what I'm talking about."

"I kind of do and I kind of don't," I said carefully. "But if you ever want to talk more, I'm here."

I missed having someone to talk to.

Clare hesitated and made a strange face. "I saw you disappear at Aquatopia, you know."

I felt myself pale. I thought she'd seen me, but there was nothing I could do about it. Did Clare know about the retake because of me? The one rule of time travel in movies was you weren't supposed to tell anyone else you were doing it. Well, that, and also not to go back in time and change anything in the first place, but that ship had sailed. I laughed nervously. "Disappeared? You mean left early. I had a headache and hung out in the cabana the rest of the day. That's why I didn't see you again."

Clare started tripping over her own words, unable to form her thoughts. "No. I saw you in the changing room. One minute you were there, and the next you just faded away. I know it sounds crazy, but it's almost as if you were . . . I mean, you couldn't be, but it looked like you were . . . I was just wondering if . . ."

I couldn't let Clare finish that sentence. If Clare knew about the app, she'd definitely try to get it and use it herself, and who knew what would happen then? My life was spiraling out of control, and I didn't know how to stop it.

"People don't just disappear!" I said with a laugh. *Except me.* "I should go find Laura so I can get to school. Don't want to be late the first day. See you there!" I opened the door and quickly shut it behind me.

My phone beeped again. Twelve percent! There was no more time to waste. If I was going to attempt another retake, it had to be now. But where did I go to do it? I couldn't let anyone else see me. I spotted a door across the hall and opened it fast. It was a storage closet. I stepped inside, turned on the light, and pushed myself up against several cases of paper towels. The door had no lock. What if someone came in? What if Clare followed me?

My phone made a weird warning beep again. Nine percent!

Would the app still work with so little power left? It had to! I couldn't stay here. But where was I traveling back to now? I'd tried looking cool at the sleepover with Laura's friends, and that backfired. Then I tried making Laura look good in front of Jake to make her happy, and now I was in a reality where I still wasn't worthy. How did I convince Laura that our friendship was worth fighting for? I needed to find a moment when it was just the two of us— no sleepovers, no water parks—and really show her how amazing our friendship is. But when was the last time we did that? I opened the Retake and started scrolling backward. The group of pictures had only grown since the last time I looked. Finally, I landed on something that looked familiar. Laura and I had taken a selfie in front of a giant white poster board that said URBAN AGRICULTURE.

Laura had hashtagged the picture #futurecityready!, which I'd reposted.

Our Future City club had made it to the finals for our district and had to do a presentation of our urban development plan at a Long Island competition. The winner went on to the regional competition. Each person in our club had a part to work on, and somehow, I got stuck giving the oral presentation. Laura had come over the weekend before to help me run through my part of the speech. I remembered us hanging out all day. She might have even slept over. I could still see us burning popcorn in my microwave and cracking up over something my dad was watching on TV. It wasn't a big moment, but it was ours alone.

Maybe I had to stop thinking of big events and concentrate on a time when we were just being Laura and Zoe. This could be that moment. I could show her I wasn't a baby and that I could still be cool and fun, even if I didn't like a boy as much as she liked Jake. This time it had to work. I clicked on the retake button, closed my eyes, and waited for the magic to happen.

Someone pounded on the door, making me open my eyes and jump.

"Anyone in there? Is this the bathroom? Emergency! Too much coffee!" a guy shouted.

My phone whined again. My charge was down to 5 percent! Why was it draining so fast now? And why was I still here? Was the app still working? I felt my mouth go dry as I started to panic. Quickly, I made my plea to the universe: "I wish I could retake this picture of Laura and me working on the Future City presentation and show her how great our friendship really is."

My heart was pounding, my forehead was sweating, and I had an overwhelming sense of dread as I stared at the app and waited for my chance to make things right. *Please don't let me be stuck here. Please!*

Just as I was about to give up, I saw familiar flash, and everything around me faded away.

CHAPTER FIFTEEN

"Zoe, move in closer. I can't see the poster board!"

Laura was giggling so hard, I couldn't understand her, but I did know what was important.

The retake had worked again.

This time I had to get things right.

Laura squeezed me tighter, trying to fit the poster and the two of us into her selfie. Finally, I saw the shot line up perfectly, and she clicked on the camera button. The light reflected off my eyes and I blinked, trying to get a grip on my surroundings. We were in my room, and music was playing softly from my wireless speaker. My bed was unmade, and there were scraps of corrugated paper all over my bedroom floor, along with glue bottles and a paint kit on a folding table. My trusty glue gun was sitting in its holder, just waiting to be used.

"Okay, now that we've pretended to be ready with this

poster, we need to actually get it done," Laura said with a laugh. "Help me color in the bubble letters." I heard her phone ping. "Hang on. I have to see who this is." She started backing out of my room. "I'll be right back. I'm just going to go out on your front steps. I'll explain later!" she said, and disappeared.

I didn't care who Laura was on the phone with. All I cared about was that my phone still worked. I looked around the room and found it charging on my bedside table. The little green battery light was illuminated, and the phone was up to 50 percent charged. I scrolled through the apps and found the fluorescent pink app illuminated. I breathed a sigh of relief and hugged the warm phone to my chest.

"You love your phone enough to hug it, huh?" Mom was standing in my doorway, watching me.

"I thought it died," I said. "It's been running really hot." Why did I just tell her that?

"Really? Let me see." Mom walked in, grabbing random shoes and discarded clothes off the floor. My room was a mess.

"I'm sure it's fine." I held tight to the phone.

"Can I see it?" Mom put her hand out and I had no choice but to hand it over. She frowned. "Wow, it is warm. Did you leave it out in the sun?"

"Nope. I'm sure it's just from being plugged in overnight." I reached for it, but Mom wouldn't let go.

"Maybe I should take it to the store to be looked at," she said. "We don't want it blowing up or anything."

"Phones don't just explode." *Do they?* I wondered. "I'm sure it's just from being plugged in too long."

Mom looked at me. "Please don't tell me you're becoming addicted to your phone like Laura is. Dianne said she sleeps with it next to her on her pillow and answers texts all night long."

Those texts weren't from me. They were probably from the drama queens about boys, kissing, and makeup. They were things I really wasn't familiar with yet, and the girls and Laura thought I was a weirdo because of it. I felt the tears coming, and this time I couldn't stop them.

"Oh, Zo-Zo, what's wrong?" Mom sat down beside me and placed the phone on the bedside table. For once, she didn't say anything about the fact my bed wasn't made (she hated unmade beds even more than she hated food left on plates in the kitchen sink). She pushed my hair off my forehead. "Are you feeling okay?"

"No." I wiped the tears away from my eyes, but more kept falling. I needed to make them stop before Laura got back.

I wished I could tell Mom about the Retake app and how it just showed up on my phone, and what I'd been trying to do, but I had the feeling she'd think I was delusional and march me to the doctor. I was in so deep with this app that I didn't even know how to stop myself. The more I tried to change the past, the more I destroyed the future. I needed to talk to someone before I exploded. But, like always, there was no time. "I just feel like everything is changing faster and faster, and there is nothing I can do to stop it."

Mom nodded. "Middle school can be tough—"

"This isn't about middle school." I didn't mean to cut her off. I glanced at the door to make sure Laura wasn't coming. "It's about Laura." Mom turned her whole body toward me to listen, her knees touching my knees. "We've been kind of in a weird place lately, and I don't know how to fix things without making them worse." I wasn't even sure how to explain it. "Nothing I do is ever right."

"Ah, honey. I love Laura—she's practically a third daughter—but friendships change over time. Just because you're not best friends every moment of every day doesn't mean you're not still friends. No matter what happens with the two of you, you'll always have amazing memories." Mom stood up and went to my corkboard, which was overflowing with pictures I recognized since nothing had technically been altered yet. "Look at all the incredible things you've done together! No one can take those moments away from you."

Well, technically, the Retake app could.

"You are who you are because of how you've grown together, but it's okay to grow apart too."

But I didn't want to grow apart from Laura. Was it wrong

to want to keep things exactly as they were? I wanted it to be me and Laura against the world, telling ghost stories in my tree house, shooting whipped cream from the can into each other's mouths instead of on our ice cream sundaes, and playing Tenzi at my dining room table on a Saturday night. We'd always been so happy together.

"I just wish we still liked the same things," I said, listening carefully to make sure Laura wasn't coming up the stairs. "I think she feels Future City is dorky."

Mom made a face. "Dorky? Finding ways to design cities that include spaces for urban agriculture is not dorky. It's helping your planet. I watched this news clip the other night about a group of Future City kids who created a water filtration system that is being used in the Dominican Republic. Many of these people had access to clean water from the tap for the first time." Mom cocked her head to one side. "If that's dorky, then I want to be a dork."

I thought of the club again and how much fun we had designing buildings and trying to solve real-world problems. I didn't love presenting, but I loved the competition. Did I really want to give Future City up for Laura? No.

Mom was right. Maybe Laura and I didn't have to do everything together, but we did have to put our friendship first. I had a feeling if we could finally have the heart-to-heart we needed, we could find a way to grow and change together instead of getting pulled apart. "Me too," I said.

Mom went to the door, leaving it ajar when she left. "Let me know if you two need anything."

"Thanks, Mom." Laura was taking forever. Who was she talking to, anyway? I went back to my phone to text her and dropped it in surprise. It was practically burning now. I grabbed it with the bottom of my shirt, and read the message on the screen. There was a tiny picture of a thermometer.

Temperature! Phone needs to cool down before you can use it.

This wasn't good. Even with the new charge, there was a chance the Retake app was going to destroy my phone. I needed to finish things with Laura and get rid of this app before I got stuck in a reality I didn't want to be in.

"I am not throwing away my shot!" I heard Laura singing as she ran up the stairs. (Her dad had recently surprised her with tickets to see *Hamilton,* and she sang the soundtrack all day long.) "Sorry about that!" she said, but didn't explain who she'd been talking to or what the call had been about.

"That's okay," I told her. "But now we get down to work," I said, trying to be funny, but I was in a time crunch here.

"Okay. Time to be serious." Laura tried to keep a straight

face but couldn't. "Sorry! I'm just in the best mood. Did I show you my tattoos?"

"You got a tattoo?" I freaked.

"They're temporary, silly." Laura thrust out her right arm. "We did them at the wrap party for the play. That's a henna tattoo of the Stinky Cheese Man, and this one is of Cinderella's glass slipper, and . . ."

The sixth-grade play was *The Stinky Cheese Man and Other Fairly Stupid Tales*. Laura had played Cinderella and Princess 2. I'd run lines with her in my bedroom and gone to see the show both nights. Laura, no surprise, had been really good.

"I wish you could have been at the party," Laura said. "It was so much fun. Ava Sinclair's parents let her have it at their house, which is huge! Her pool looks like the one at that Coconut Point resort."

That explained Laura's pool posts. "The one with the rock walls?"

"We didn't swim because her parents had just opened the pool that weekend, and I had my hair up from the Cinderella costume, but it looked like the best pool ever. We have to get an invitation to go over to Ava's," Laura said.

But I didn't want to waste time talking about Ava. The clock was ticking, and today could be my last shot.

"Earth to Zo-Zo! Come in, Zo-Zo!" Laura was waving a hand in front of my face.

My thoughts snapped back to the (current) present. "Sorry."

Laura leaned back on my bed and picked up a stuffed manatee. "I can't believe you still have these."

The word "baby" flashed in my mind. I had about a dozen stuffed animals that resided on my bed. We got most of them together. As much as I wasn't ready to give up Sir Moosington, maybe it was time. "I'm tossing them this weekend," I lied. "Middle school is too old for stuffed animals. No offense."

"Oh, mine are gone too." Laura tossed Manny the Manatee aside. "I just thought you weren't answering me because you were daydreaming about Kyle Evans." She sat up on her knees and looked at me. "He's so cute. Not Jake Graser cute, but you said you loved watching him pretend to be Jack from Jack and the Beanstalk. So are you going to talk to him?"

I had meant his acting. But if I didn't say I liked a real boy—meaning anyone other than the professional German soccer player whose picture hung on my wall—then Laura would think I was immature. "Oh, he's totally cute. He has a great voice too."

"I knew it!" Laura grabbed the throw pillow on my bed that said "Beach, Sleep, Repeat" and hugged it. "Why didn't you tell me? I could have asked him if he liked you during the wrap party."

"Uh . . ." I didn't want to wake up in the future and have broken up with yet another boy I didn't remember dating. When I had my first kiss, I wanted it to be for real. "That's okay." Better to change the subject. "But what about you and Jake?"

She threw herself back onto my bed. "Jake just talked to his friends and painted props during play practice. He never even spoke to me, and he didn't go to the wrap party either."

"His loss."

Laura's phone chirped—she'd recently changed her message sound to birds chirping—and she read the text, then burst out laughing.

"What?" I said.

"Nothing. It's stupid." She put her phone down again. Her phone continued chirping. It sounded like we were in a bird sanctuary. "Okay, where are your flash cards? I want to hear your part of the presentation." Her phone chirped again. Laura quickly texted someone.

"Who's texting you?" I asked. "Kyle Evans?"

Laura clutched her phone to her heart. "No! I want Jake to text me so badly! We have to figure out how to sit near him on the bus for Aquatopia next week."

"Uh, yeah." I did not want to think about Aquatopia again. "Okay. Why don't I read my part, and then you can read yours? I memorized my half."

"Impressive! You're a true actress. Hit it!"

"Okay." I stood up straight and cleared my throat, then

looked down at the flash cards. "When we set out to figure out where we could create an aquaponic farm, we looked to Bushwick, in New York, where Oko Farms is doing just that—cultivating freshwater fish while also growing fruits and . . . fruits and . . . uh . . ." I seemed to be missing the next card, and it had been a while since I'd rehearsed this. "I need to practice the rest."

"That was good! You didn't need my help at all. You never do," Laura said.

"That's not true." Was it?

Laura shrugged. "I just mean you've got this down. We don't need the practice."

"Oh, I need the practice," I lied. What if she tried to leave already? "I'm really stressed about tomorrow."

"When I'm stressed over my lines, I play music," Laura said. "Alexa! Play today's top hits." Immediately, a song we both knew filled the air and we started singing along. "I'm dying to dance to this song with Jake!"

"Oh my God, all you talk about is Jake!" I said, laughing at the absurdity of it. I was sort of glad I didn't like anyone that much yet. It seemed like a lot of work. I still couldn't believe I dated him in another reality.

"Because he's so cute!" Laura said, and her phone chirped again. "Hey. What are you wearing tomorrow? All the girls from the play are going to the mall, and I lied and said we had a family thing so I didn't have to tell them we were going to a Future City competition."

I stopped dancing. "Why do you care what they think? We're changing the world here. Or we could be."

Laura rolled her eyes. "Don't get all dramatic about it. I just said I didn't want people to know. I'm still going."

"You're allowed to do your own thing, you know."

"Ooh! I love this song!" Laura ignored me and started singing a Taylor Swift song at the top of her lungs. "Remember when we made up that routine to that Shawn Mendes song?"

I couldn't help but smile at the memory. "Yes. We practiced it every day for weeks. You were convinced if we sent it to Shawn, he'd repost it on Instagram and we'd be famous." I started giggling.

"I still think he would have if you learned how to do a handstand," Laura said accusingly.

"I can barely balance on two feet! You wanted me to balance on my hands! It was never going to happen!"

Laura stuffed a pretzel into her mouth and almost choked, she was laughing so hard. "Even though you can dive for a volleyball and save the shot with no problem? How can the same person not do a handstand?"

"I just can't," I insisted as she tossed me two pretzels, like she already knew I wanted some.

"Yes, you can! Let's try that handstand again now." Laura pushed the craft table out of the way, making an aisle of carpet in my room.

"You're serious?"

"Yes, I'm serious," Laura said, even though she was laughing. "Alexa! Play 'If I Can't Have You' by Shawn Mendes!" It immediately started playing. "Try it!"

I joined her on the carpet.

"Five, six, seven, eight," Laura called out, and I joined in, matching her steps till we hit the first chorus and the handstand. We were both laughing so hard that we had trouble concentrating. Laura nailed it. I tripped and fell into the lamp on my bedside table, knocking it off and sending my phone flying. The resulting sound was loud.

"My phone!" I cried.

"What's going on up there?" I heard my dad yell from downstairs.

"Dropped something! Sorry, Mr. M!" Laura shouted as I went to check on my phone.

The hot temperature reading was gone. The phone was still warm but not burning. I clicked on Retake, and the pink icon was still there. "That could have been bad," I whispered.

Laura popped over my shoulder. "Hey. What's that pink app on your phone?"

CHAPTER SIXTEEN

Without thinking, I hid my phone behind my back and tried to control my breathing. "It's some stupid game Taryn told me to download."

"What stupid game did I tell you to download?" Taryn leaned on my door. She was holding a bowl of popcorn. Laura went over and took a handful of it. "I don't download games."

Laura and Taryn were staring curiously at me now, but I didn't know what to say. I couldn't let anyone else know about the Retake app.

I placed the phone in my back pocket, warming my butt. "It's nothing. I haven't even played it."

Laura and Taryn looked at each other.

"If she won't tell you, she definitely won't tell me." Taryn walked away.

I winced at the dig. "Not true! I love my sister!"

Laura's phone continued to chirp, and she looked at it again. "Hey. How long do you think this practice session will take?"

"I don't know." I didn't remember Laura being in such a rush the first time. My whole brain felt foggy trying to keep track of every conversation we'd now had over the last few days, in the past, the present, and what I remembered of the original past. I remembered the chirping cell phone because it had driven me nuts. Laura had eventually changed the ringtone to a swoosh sound. But pushing for us to finish faster, I didn't remember. I guess it wasn't the most exciting afternoon. That gave me an idea. "Hey. Want to sleep over tonight? It's warm enough to sleep in the tree house. Then we can both practice our parts of the presentation several times." Laura's phone chirped again. "You have got to change that ringtone."

"You're right. I'm going to hear chirping in my sleep. How about this?" Laura pressed some buttons, and I heard the familiar swoosh of the past.

"Much better."

"Good. But I can't sleep over tonight." Laura frowned. "I'm not even sure I can stay long. My mom is texting me like crazy. My dad and her are switching weekends because he has to go away for work next weekend, so she has to take us over there this afternoon. I can probably eke out another hour."

"Oh. Okay." I tried not to sound disappointed. How was

I going to get through to Laura within the hour? "I can practice later on my own then, so we have more time to hang."

"No, you wanted me to come over to practice, so let's hear you go again from the top." She took a handful of chips.

"Okay." I cleared my throat and started to speak. Laura burst out laughing.

"You are too cute. Let's take a selfie." She grabbed her phone and held it up. "Say 'BFFs'!"

"You're nuts."

"That's not what I said to say."

"Fine. 'BFFs.'"

Laura snapped the picture and threw the phone down onto my bed. "Pee break!" she declared. "I'll be right back." She headed out into the hall again, and Taryn appeared as if by magic.

"Can you guys shut the door if you're going to blast Shawn Mendes? He's kind of over."

"If he's so over, why did you go to his concert with us a few months ago?" I challenged.

Taryn's cheeks reddened. "The tickets were a gift. I didn't want to be rude."

The swoosh sound blared through the room, then went off two more times.

"Who is blowing up Laura's phone?" Taryn asked, picking up her phone.

"Hey!" I reached for the phone. "Don't read Laura's texts!"

"I read yours, but yours are all Pinterest links and weird emojis. But Laura's . . ." Taryn looked at me. "Who is the Stinky Cheese Squad?"

"The Stinky Cheese Squad?" I wasn't sure. "That has to be people from the play."

"They're on some big group text," Taryn said. "Something about a sleepover at some girl Ava's house? Because she has a heated pool? And the boys might come for a night swim? What boys? Your number isn't on this group text." Taryn gave me a sharp look. "Is she trying to ditch you?"

I grabbed the phone and looked at Laura's last text: "Trying to get out of here and come!" she'd written. My heart sank, and that was before I read the other comments.

"Good!" Ava had written. "Tell Geekarella you have to go already and get over here!"

"LOL!" Hyacinth had written, and several others had sent laughing emojis.

The worst part was that Laura had texted a laughing emoji back too.

Not only was Laura ditching me, she was making fun of me to fit in with her new friends. I wasn't sure what stung more—that they had so much to say about me when they barely knew me or that Laura was agreeing with them.

Now I felt stupid. I had picked this moment because I thought the afternoon had been about two besties hanging out together. But it turned out Laura had been texting the girls the whole time, trying to find an excuse to leave. I wasn't sure if I should laugh or cry at how stupid I'd been. Laura had lied about going to her dad's, no less. My house had pretzels, a glue gun, and stuffed animals that Laura felt were babyish. Ava's house had a pool that belonged at a hotel, and cute boys who might show up. In Laura's eyes I couldn't compete.

It didn't matter that I was the friend who helped her through her parents' divorce, or the one who checked on her at the first-aid station when she scraped her knee at a water park, or the girl who threw her an epic party every year for her birthday. Laura wanted to move on, and I was starting to see there was nothing I could do to stop her.

"As usual, you're right about Laura," I said, my voice suddenly hoarse. "I guess I just didn't want to see it before now. She's moved on without me."

I looked down at my phone. It was sizzling to the touch, the new selfie of Laura and me frozen on the screen. The picture may have been different, but the result was the same. I was tired. I wanted to go home, back to my present. But when I used Retake to get myself back, what would I find waiting for me? This time the drama queens and Laura obviously wouldn't be part of my life. Did that mean I'd be alone?

Taryn's face softened. "Oh Zoe." And for the first time

in a long time, she reached out and hugged me. I hugged her right back.

"Hey." Laura stood in the doorway, looking anxious. "Everything okay?"

Taryn pulled away and looked at me. "You've got this," she whispered.

"What's going on?" Laura asked.

I tried to calm down, but I couldn't. My best friend—the one I shared markers with in first grade and clothes with in fifth, who I sang every song with in the car and who I told all my most important secrets to—didn't want to be my best friend anymore. She felt bad about it at first, I guessed, which was why she was lying that afternoon, but the truth was something the app couldn't show. Captions and hashtags didn't tell the whole story. They didn't even tell the real story a lot of the time. Laura preferred her new friends over me, and there was nothing I could do to change that. To her, I was Geekarella.

"Zo-Zo. Are you okay?"

Unless . . .

"I have to tell you something," I said, my heart beating wildly.

"What's wrong?" Laura reached for the manatee she supposedly hated and held it on her lap. "Everything okay?" Her phone made the swoosh sound again. She grabbed it and placed it in her lap. "If this is about the texts—"

I cut her off. I didn't think. I didn't second-guess my-self. I didn't even rehearse what I was going to say. "Ava, Marisol, Sarah, and the girls from the play aren't really your friends."

"What?" Laura's face froze. "Did you look at my phone? Listen, about today—"

"That's not it. I heard them talking yesterday when my mom took Taryn and me out for pizza," I lied, thinking fast. "They were at A Slice of Heaven, and I heard them making fun of you in the bathroom."

Laura's face fell. "What did they say?"

"That Jake would never like you, but they wanted you to think that he might so that they could make a fool of you in front of him at some pool party."

"Ava's pool party is tonight," Laura said, suddenly ad-mitting it. She was squeezing my manatee so hard, he had a squished face.

"They said the boys were going to make you look bad because Ava wants Jake for herself." My heart beat faster as Laura's eyes welled with tears.

"Ava said that?" Laura whispered. "She told me she liked Shardul."

"I guess she said that so you wouldn't be mad." The word vomit was coming up faster now, and I couldn't stop it. I just kept piling it on. "Marisol said you think you're such a great actress when you're not, and Steph agreed and said you don't have a good voice. And then Sarah said you'll never make the middle school play next year. Ava was talking about them all trying out for this summer play— *Annie,* I think—and not telling you about it because they don't want to do it with you." Laura looked like she might burst into tears, but I kept going. "I wasn't going to tell you, but we're best friends, and best friends tell each other the truth."

You're a liar, a voice in my head said, but I pushed it way down where I couldn't hear it.

"I can't believe them," Laura said softly, tears running down her face. "I was going to invite them to my pre-summer sleepover party. I thought they were my friends."

And I thought you were mine. I tried to block out the texts Laura had sent making fun of me to the group, but I kept seeing the laughing-face emoji. I had to chalk it up to her wanting to fit in, just like I was trying to do.

"I didn't even know there was a summer theater pro-duction of *Annie!* I can't believe they didn't tell me they were auditioning."

They didn't tell you because they don't know about the show yet. It won't be announced till the first week of July. But Laura didn't know the future like I did.

"I feel like such a fool," Laura said. "To think . . . I have to tell you something too." Her eyes were big and wide. "I said I was going to my dad's, but I was really going to Ava's later."

I tried to slow my breathing, but my heart kept

thumping in my chest so loud I was sure Laura would hear it. I felt so guilty. "Oh." That's about the only word I could manage.

"I tried to get them to invite you—I've told them about you, but they don't know you, and I didn't want to make you feel bad by telling you I had plans. I just really liked all of them and wanted to be their friend. I was hoping they'd be yours too, but they're a pretty tight group."

"Oh," I said again, because now I felt even worse. I wondered if that's what had happened that day at the cabana too. I hadn't realized Laura tried to bring me into the group. Not that I wanted to be friends with those girls—I knew that now from all my retakes with them—but at least Laura hadn't fully given up on us right away. She'd tried. I just hadn't known it.

I was pretty sure I was going to throw up.

Laura hugged me. "I can't believe I was going to ditch my best friend for those girls. I'm so sorry, Zo-Zo."

I held on tight. *I'm sorry too,* I thought, *but not sorry enough to tell you the truth.*

CHAPTER SEVENTEEN

That night Laura wound up sleeping over.

It was her idea. "We have some catching up to do," she'd said. "I feel like I haven't seen you in ages."

That was probably because she hadn't.

This was the moment I'd wanted Retake to give me all along, but I hadn't seen it in any post. There were no pictures as proof. Laura had turned her phone off and put it in her bag hours ago, after declaring she never wanted to speak to any of the girls from the play again.

We slept in the tree house, the two of us in matching sleeping bags, a wireless speaker playing softly beside our lantern, which glowed as we talked for hours about summer being around the corner. It felt like fifth grade again, and all the years before it. I should have been thrilled, but the knot in my stomach continued to grow.

None of this felt real.

"Come with me to Lake George," Laura said suddenly. "Dad said I could bring you."

"He did? You never told me that," I realized, my eyes growing sleepy.

Laura sat up on one elbow. She was wearing a pair of my pajamas since she'd never gone home. "How could I? My dad just told me that I could this morning."

"Right." I held tight to the phone at my side, praying it wouldn't burst into flames.

Laura was giving me exactly what I wanted—more time—but the nagging voice in the back of my head kept reminding me why: I had lied to keep my best friend. I had sunk her new friendships to keep Laura exactly where I wanted her, by my side. And it felt wrong.

"So you'll come?" Laura asked again. "We get back the day before you leave, I think, and if not, I'm sure your mom and dad will leave a day late so that you can go away with me. It will be fun. There are these arcades that we go to at night when we walk around town, and . . ."

But I'd stopped listening, instead just saying "uh-huh" and "yeah" every so often when Laura paused. After a while, Laura stopped talking. I listened to the sounds of crickets softly chirping outside the tree house and the occasional car rumble by on a nearby street. Eventually, I heard her snoring.

I did it.

I'd annihilated the drama queens.

Laura and I were still best friends.

I'd gotten exactly what I wanted.

So why did I feel so miserable?

The truth was eating away at me. I couldn't stay here a minute longer. I pulled out my phone, feeling the back of it burn my fingertips as I held it in my hand. I clicked on the app. It opened on a selfie of Laura and me and allowed me to scroll through pictures once more. I searched for one from the second attempt at the first day of school my dad took and found the new picture of us standing side by side on my front lawn.

I'd hashtagged it #seventhgradeherewecome. We were both smiling, but even in that reality, something about the picture felt off. I'm sure it was all the guilt I had about manipulating the past to make my present dreams come true.

Maybe I really did need to grow up a bit. Not because Laura wanted me to be someone I wasn't, but because I couldn't lie to hold on to what I wanted. If Laura and I were meant to be best friends in the future, then it wouldn't matter if we liked different things. We'd find our own ways back to each other.

My finger hovered over the button that would take me back to the present. I looked over at Laura sleeping. *I'll make it up to you,* I vowed. *I'll be the best friend ever, and we'll put this whole thing behind us.* "I want to go back to the present," I whispered, hoping Laura wouldn't wake up. Then I clicked on the new picture of us and waited for the flash.

There was a blinding light, and before I knew it, the world around me faded away.

CHAPTER EIGHTEEN

"Did you get the picture? We're going to be late!"

There were lots of voices as I blinked hard, the flash of light blinding me. Laura was standing nearby checking her phone.

"Zoe! Where is your backpack?" Mom asked. "Did you leave it in your room? Dianne is swinging back around in a moment to take you guys to school. One of the twins forgot her lunch box, so she ran home."

"Uh . . ." How did I know? I scanned the front lawn. I didn't see it anywhere. "I think I left it on my desk. I'll run upstairs and grab it." I took the steps two at a time and reached my room. At least I thought it was my room. The bag was sitting on my bed, but my teal comforter had been replaced by a yellow one, and my stuffed animals had disappeared along with my cute German soccer player poster. The walls were pretty much bare except for the corkboard, still hanging over my desk. I walked over to look at it.

The pictures were all of me and Laura from this past summer. Laura and me on a boat! Laura and me side by side on paddleboards! Laura and me sleeping in the tree house under twinkle lights! I scanned the rest of the photos, looking to see who else was in them, but there was no one but me and Laura. No Reagan, Jada, or Clare. No drama queens. It was just the two of us against the world, as it always had been. I reached for my phone. The phone was charged to 100 percent. That was good news too. I pulled open the app and scrolled through my feed. There were a zillion pictures of Laura and me at the cabana, swimming in the pool, boogie boarding in the ocean, hanging out in the backyard. We'd documented every moment of our summer together with lots of BFF hashtags.

Everything was exactly the way I wanted it.

I grabbed my bag and headed downstairs. Mom was waiting. "Let's go! Laura is already in the car."

"Okay." I said, and gave her a kiss. At least we weren't fighting this time around.

"And please find something to do after school today, okay?" Mom added. "There's got to be one club on the list you and Laura are willing to try."

Huh? "I have volleyball tryouts today," I told her as I opened the door. "And I'm sticking with Future City."

Mom looked puzzled. "You quit the club last June. And volleyball tryouts started already. You didn't want to go."

"No, they start today," I said, my heart beating fast.

"Coach started them yesterday and you didn't want to be there. Dumb move," Taryn said, bouncing down the stairs behind me. "First, you give up Future City, which you always loved, then Laura says no volleyball, and suddenly it's no volleyball."

These were my two favorite things to do. If Laura and I were good, why would I give them up? What was I taking now? Tennis? I was terrible at tennis. Lacrosse? "Please don't tell me I'm playing lacrosse."

"Why would you play lacrosse?" Taryn asked. "Don't tell me this is part of your and Laura's we-will-only-do-things-together pact. Mom, can you tell her to quit it with this?"

"Taryn, don't start." Mom looked at me. "I think it's great you and Laura have each other, but you have to find an activity you both will like and go to a meeting immediately, or you're doing one on your own. You hear me?" Dianne honked her car horn.

"Yes." We had no activities? That sounded pretty boring.

"Have a great first day!" Mom said, waving to Dianne before closing the door behind me.

I hesitated slightly before sticking my head in the air-conditioned car. Paige and Petra were in the second row, and Laura was in the front seat.

"Zoe!" Paige sounded excited. The twins were wearing

matching tees and shorts, and both had their hair in pigtails. When you're seven, that sort of thing is acceptable. "When are you coming over again?"

"She's over every day, Paige," Petra said. "She lives at the house."

"She doesn't *live* at the house. It just feels like it because Mom says they have no other friends." I winced.

"Paige." Dianne's voice had an edge. "Sorry I had to run back to the house. You guys will still be on time, even though you would have been early if you'd just taken the bus." Laura rolled her eyes. "I was just telling Laura you two have to find a club to join."

"Mom." Laura sighed heavily.

"What? You two aren't doing Future City, volleyball, or trying out for the play. I don't understand what's going on! You loved the sixth-grade play last spring! I can't believe you don't want to audition again."

"Zoe and I don't want to do the play," Laura said, sounding like my spokesperson. "And you remember what happened during the Future City presentation for our competition. She broke out in hives."

"I broke out in hives?" I squeaked. That hadn't happened last time.

Paige started to giggle. "It was really funny."

"But it's seventh grade! This is your chance to try new things."

"You sound like my mom," I said as we turned onto the block where school was.

"That's because our moms talk all the time," Laura supplied. "Like us."

"But we still get out there. We're not sitting home glued to our phones," Dianne said as she turned in to the parking lot. "We aren't afraid to take the bus."

"Mom," Laura said sharply. "Zoe and I don't want to hang out with liars."

I felt my stomach clench.

"And a lot of these sports and clubs . . . They've all got people trying out who are total mean girls. And boys."

"Mean boys," Paige repeated. "Mean boys!"

"We don't want to be around them. We'd rather be alone. We don't need new friends." She looked back at me and smiled, but I couldn't help noticing the smile was sort of sad.

So *this* is what had happened to us? We were marching behind the no-new-friends banner and we lived in an imaginary bubble I created?

"OUCH!" Paige screamed, and I saw my phone slip from her hands. "Your phone is on fire."

My phone hit the floor with a loud thud.

"Paige, what did I tell you about taking people's phones?" Dianne reprimanded as we pulled up to the school drop-off zone.

"But Zoe had it just sitting there in her bag pocket. And she has all my favorite games!" Paige glanced at me accusingly. "Why is your phone so hot?"

"'Hot'?" Dianne repeated. "Oh, Zoe, be careful with that. I just saw this segment on the news about a girl's phone blowing up in her bag."

"Mom, phones don't just blow up in their bags." Laura looked back at me worriedly. "Do they? Zo-Zo, is your phone broken?"

"No, but . . . Oh no." I looked down at the screen and noticed the spiderlike crack now spreading across it. It must have happened when Paige dropped it. "I can hardly read the screen."

"Paige!" Laura yelled at her, and Paige started to cry. She took my phone. "Ouch! This is hot. But wait!" She started peeling the corner of my screen. "Look! Your phone is fine. It was just the screen protector."

Whew! I pulled the broken screen protector off. I took the phone back and looked for the bright pink icon. It was still there. "Paige, it's fine. Don't cry." Paige looked over, and I held the phone up. "See? I can get a new screen protector after school."

"Oh good! But still, Zoe, tell your mom to take your phone in if it's running hot," Dianne said. "And I'll pay for the screen protector since it was Paige's fault."

"It's all right," I said as I stepped out of the car behind

Laura. No one was touching my phone. I slid it into the interior pocket of my bag for safekeeping.

"Have a good first day, ladies. And go to some club meetings!" Dianne pulled away. People were streaming into the school around us as buses continued to pull up.

"She will not stop about us joining stuff," Laura said with a groan. "Your mom too?"

"Yeah." I hesitated. "But they're not wrong. Why did we quit everything?"

Laura bit her lip. "You know why. We've been over the club list. There isn't one we can both agree on, and sports tryouts already started. We're out of luck for the fall."

I couldn't believe there was nothing we could agree on anymore. "That's impossible! There has to be something we both like."

"Stop," Laura snapped. "We like different things, okay? And even if you did agree to do stage crew for the musical, I'd never want to do it because of what Sarah and Ava said about me."

I felt like I had been punched in the stomach. The lie was the glue holding our friendship together. It had followed me into the future, and it had cost us both.

Laura glanced at the school warily. "I can't believe I have so many classes with Sarah. How am I going to even look at her?"

I shifted my bag uncomfortably. "It's class. You

won't have time to talk." The first bell rang. "See you at lunch?"

"We're meeting by the upstairs bathroom. Don't forget." Laura attempted a smile, but she still looked lost. I couldn't help feeling like it was all my fault. "Please tell me you brought your schedule."

I reached into my bag and found it tucked inside. "I've got it this time. I mean, today."

Laura and I walked to the doors together, flashed our student IDs that were on lanyards around our necks, and parted down separate hallways. I headed upstairs for my first class.

Laura and I both deserved to be happy, but in this reality, neither of us was. I wanted us to be best friends, but at what cost? She wasn't acting. I wasn't in Future City or volleyball. I'd messed up both of our years before they'd even started.

It was time for me to stop thinking about what I wanted and think about what was best for both of us.

I had to let go.

I blinked back tears.

Oh no. I couldn't cry on the first day of seventh grade, no matter how many times I'd done this day before. I looked around for the nearest bathroom and spotted the infamous one I'd fought with Laura in during my second retake. I slipped inside to get a tissue.

Clare was already in there. She had on a Captain Marvel tee and ripped jeans. This time her hair tips were bright green, and she had on polka-dot fashion glasses. I noticed her eyes were swollen. "Hey," she said. "I was just getting a tissue."

"Me too." Slowly, I racked my brain—did Clare remember helping me in the bathroom that time I had the fight with Laura? Or hanging out with me at Aquatopia and talking about our favorite book? Or asking me about my disappearing act in the bagel store bathroom? Or helping me navigate classes on the real first day of school? I wasn't sure how my timeline worked anymore, but I was pretty sure all those memories I had of Clare—including the one where she told me about her friendship with Ava—were only mine now. The rest had disappeared during the retake.

"I don't mean to get up in your business, but are you okay?" Clare asked with a concerned smile.

And that's when I remembered the one thing that had remained consistent in every memory I had of her— Clare would make a great friend. We both loved books, our STEM clubs, and trying crazy water rides. We loved to laugh and talk about everything and anything. And we both tried to be there for each other when we needed it most.

Actually . . .

That wasn't true. Clare had been there for me, but how had I helped her? Reagan and Jada convinced her to hang out at the water park, but I was too busy chasing Laura to invite her. And when Clare asked me about the app in the bagel store bathroom, I bolted instead of letting her in on my secret. I wasn't trying to be selfish. Retake wasn't working the way I wanted it to. How did I know it wouldn't mess up Clare's life as badly as it had messed up mine?

Friendship wasn't a one-way street. What I'd done to Laura by lying was cruel. If she was truly my friend, she would have wanted to keep me in her life. But Clare was different. We kept running into each other, and I wondered if there was a reason why. Maybe we were always meant to be friends, and I'd failed to see it till now. If that was true, I didn't want to risk making the same mistakes with her that I had with Laura. If I wanted to be Clare's friend, I couldn't just take. I needed to give too. Retake might not have helped me, but I might be able to use it to do something for Clare. I looked at the peeling paint in the bathroom and wondered.

"I'm fine, but do you want to sit together at lunch today?" I asked suddenly. "I think we both have lunch fifth period."

Clare smiled. "Uh, yeah. Sure."

"Okay," I repeated, and we stood there smiling. Then the first bell rang.

Clare moved to the door. "Are you coming? I think we have math together."

"I'll catch up with you." Clare nodded and slipped out the door.

I pulled the phone out of my bag and looked at the pink icon again. I'd come close to breaking my phone once already, and it was still running really hot. What if this was my last chance to make things right?

Then I had to use the retake to do something good.

I might not have been able to fix things with Laura, but maybe I could keep Clare from wasting sixth-grade hanging out in this dreary bathroom.

Quickly, I started scrolling through the app. I wasn't sure if there was a picture that would work for what I needed to do. Clare had said she and Ava got to sixth grade and things were already bad between them, so I needed a picture from school that got me as close to the start of sixth grade as possible. After endless scrolling, I landed on one of me and Laura in the middle school hallway. We were wearing royal blue, and our hair was sprayed the same color. We had our arms wrapped around each other and matching blue tattoos on our left cheeks. I had written #wevegotspirit #fairviewms. Spirit week was the second week of school!

I went to click on the Retake arrow and stopped. Before I skipped to that moment, I needed to find a way to get back to this one later. I opened my camera and smiled, then I clicked a selfie of myself and posted it. Quickly, I wrote #firstday, hoping the picture uploaded. When it did, I scrolled back to the spirit week photo and clicked on the back arrow.

"Here goes nothing. Please let me go back to spirit week and make things right." The phone was almost too hot to hold at this point, but I kept staring into it and waited for the flash.

The next moment I was standing with my arms wrapped around Laura.

People all around us were screaming and cheering.

"We won!" Laura shouted. "Isn't it amazing? Fairview never wins the homecoming game!" People were throwing pom-poms and paper airplanes and high-fiving.

I looked around to see where we were. Second floor. Good. The bathroom was just down the hall. My heart started to beat faster.

"Selfie!" Laura said, pulling me in tighter. "Say 'Fairview'!"

"Fairview!" I pulled away and really looked at my best friend for a moment. This was us in our prime, back when we were still each other's whole friendship world. I could be sad, and I was, but I also needed to remember what Mom said—I'd always have the memories. "I'll meet you back here!" I shouted over Dougie's chant of "Fairview!" in the background. "I forgot something at my locker."

"Okay!" Laura shouted back, and joined the Fairview chant.

I hurried down the hall, went straight to my locker, and found what I was looking for—a pink Post-it notepad. Then I grabbed a pen and ran all the way to the bathroom. I burst through the door, half expecting to see Clare. Instead, the room was empty. Perfect.

I went to the peeling wall, and scribbled my note on the Post-it.

> *C—It gets better. I promise.—Z*

Then I thought about Clare and how she'd changed my life since she came into it, and I wrote a second note.

> *You never know where you'll meet a new friend— maybe it's in this very bathroom!*

I thought about Mom's advice too and wrote a third note.

> *If we want to grow, then we have to continue to change.*

Satisfied, I left the pad and the pen on the windowsill and stared up at the notes on the wall. It was a start. I only hoped Clare saw them and they multiplied.

Then I pulled out my phone again. "Ouch!" I said aloud. The phone wasn't going to last much longer before it overheated. I found the pink icon, opened it, located my latest selfie, and, heart pounding, clicked the retake button again. "Let's go back to the present, please." There was a bright flash, and I held my breath, afraid to see *when* I'd wind up. Then I was gone.

CHAPTER NINETEEN

I opened my eyes.

I was back in the bathroom. That was a good sign.

I felt for my hot phone and checked the date: It was the first day of school of seventh grade. Another good sign. Then I turned around and gasped.

Where there had been three pink Post-it notes, there were now hundreds covering the wall. Blue ones, green ones, teal, yellow, and glittery ones too. Some had nothing but a single word, like "hope," while others were written in such small print, I couldn't even read them. I noticed one that said "You R Awesome! (I know this for a fact!)" In the middle of the wall was a large white note:

Due to the popularity of the positivity wall, we will be painting the adjacent wall with

chalkboard paint so you can continue sharing
and caring!

It was signed "Principal Higgins." I touched the note, proud to have had a hand in this. A Post-it underneath fell off and fluttered to the ground. I picked it up. It was written in purple Sharpie in tiny, neat letters. "I put this note here for sixth-grade girls especially," it read. "Maybe you and your friends feel sad sometimes or are in pain. Don't worry. It will be okay. Smile! And branch out!"

Clare.

Could she have written this?

I could only hope she had. Or she had least seen this, and it had made a difference between her spending most of her year in a bathroom and branching out.

Now all that was left to do was to help Laura. I didn't really need the app to do that. I'd start by being honest with her, as much as it might hurt.

I had to make it to fifth period, when we had lunch. Then I could take Laura aside and convince her to join the play. I'd ask Ms. Pepper if I could rejoin Future City. And I'd find a way to make up the volleyball tryout I'd missed.

I saw Clare in class, but there was no time to talk to her to see if the positivity wall had helped her. All I knew was that her hair had changed again—this time the tips were teal.

By lunchtime I had my speech planned. I stood outside

the east cafeteria and waited for Laura to show up. Dougie came running by, and I noticed the drama queens head to a table, but there was no sign of Laura. I felt bad not sitting with Clare, but I had to take care of things. Ten minutes into the period, I risked the wrath of Principal Higgins and pulled my phone out of my pocket to see if Laura had texted. It was so warm, I had to hold it with the edges of my T-shirt.

Finally, I spotted Laura walking toward me. She wasn't smiling.

"Hey! Are you all right?" I asked, rushing over.

"No." Laura looked like she might cry. "We said we'd meet by the girls' bathroom on the second floor and walk to lunch together. You never showed up!"

Uh-oh. "I'm so sorry. I forgot."

"I felt so stupid. Sarah came by with Marisol, and they both said hi to me and asked if I was going to try out for the play, and I didn't know what to say to them." Laura pulled at her ponytail. "I couldn't understand why they were suddenly being so nice. And you weren't there."

"I'm really sorry. Let's eat," I suggested. "We can talk more then." We really needed to talk.

"I'm not hungry." Laura spied the crowded cafeteria anxiously. "I don't want to go in there."

This did not sound like Laura at all. What had I done to us? This conversation couldn't wait another moment. "I think you should try out for the play," I blurted out.

Laura looked at me strangely. "What? No. We talked about this."

"I know, but I think you should do it. You're good. And you like it! Don't not do it because I'm not."

Laura shuffled her feet anxiously. I could swear I saw her glance at the drama queens' table. "But the girls . . ."

"Maybe they'll be nicer to you now," I said. "And who cares if they're not? You deserve to be up there just like they do."

"But we made a pact," Laura said, twirling her hair around her finger as she grew more anxious. "Together or not at all. Remember? I'm not going back on that. You're my best friend for a reason. We've always been honest with each other."

Time to rip the Band-Aid off. "That isn't exactly true."

"What do you mean?" Laura asked.

"I lied to you," I said, louder than I intended. "Sarah, Ava, and the others never said you weren't a good actor or that they wanted to make a fool of you. And they weren't going to hide *Annie* auditions from you. I made it up because I didn't want you doing the musical and forgetting about me." Laura looked stunned. The cafeteria grew quiet. "I didn't want to lose our friendship." I reached out for her hand. "Laura, I'm so sorry."

Wow, it felt good getting that off my chest.

Laura yanked her hand away. "Don't talk to me!" she

shouted, and I heard Dougie go "Ooh!" as she turned and ran down the hall.

"Laura!" I finally caught up to her when we were at the stairs leading to the basement. "Let me explain!" I hurried alongside her. "It all started when I was looking at pictures of us from last year. Like this one. Look!" I pulled the phone out of my bag again, feeling it burn my fingers. I tried to show her my screensaver—the two of us standing in front of our cabana. "Look!" I shoved the phone in front of her.

"I don't want to look at your phone!" Laura's hand came flying up and swiped mine, knocking the phone out of my hands.

The two of us watched in horror as the phone hit a step with a thunderous bang, then bounced several steps before it landed faceup. Even from where I was standing, I could see that the screen was cracked.

"NO!" I cried, rushing down the steps to grab it. I picked it up. The phone was glitching. For a split second I saw Retake open and land on the picture of Laura and me from this morning, on my front lawn. Then the screen went dark, and the phone died in my hands. When I looked up, Laura was gone.

CHAPTER TWENTY

Never have a fight in front of everyone in front of the cafeteria.

I learned that lesson the hard way.

By sixth period everyone knew Laura and I had had a fight, but no one seemed to know why, since neither of us was talking. Clare and I didn't have afternoon classes together, and Jada and Reagan were nice enough not to ask, but by seventh period, Dougie was giving people the scoop, having apparently followed us out of the cafeteria. He didn't know *why* we were yelling, but he did see Laura supposedly *throw* my phone down the stairs, where it broke.

By eighth period I overheard someone say we were fighting over Jake Graser. Then the girl behind that person said we were fighting because I posted an unflattering picture of Laura online. I would have told both those haters that neither story was true, but then I'd have to say what really happened: that I'd used an app to somehow redo moments from the past to save our friendship.

And every time I tried to go back and make things better between us, I only made things worse. That my phone was now broken, trapping me in a reality that was somehow worse than the one I started with. Sure, Laura and I weren't BFFs in my old reality, but at least she didn't seem to hate me. The way things were now, there was no chance of her being my Christiane Larken, like my mom had. We were worse than broken. We were done.

And now my phone was destroyed too, holding me hostage in this reality forever.

Hold it together, Zoe, I told myself, but when the bell rang at the end of school, and someone came over the loudspeaker reminding people about tryouts, meetings, and not to forget bus passes, I realized I had a bigger problem: I had no way home.

There was no way I was going to show up for a ride from Dianne after what I'd done.

And when I searched my bag, there was no bus pass. Added problem: No phone meant no way to call Mom to tell her I'd be walking home. I had no choice but to go back to the dreaded main office and ask to use their phone.

The halls were just as crowded after school as they were during and I worried about running into Laura. She would probably stick around till after club period ended—Dianne had practically insisted on it—so there was a good chance I'd see her, and I didn't know if that was good or bad. When I passed a sign for the drama club, I saw Ava and Hyacinth reading the flyer.

"Meeting about the play is in room 228," I heard Ava say. I hoped Laura would be there.

"How's your phone?" Dougie yelled when I passed him and a pack of boys.

I needed air. I ducked into one of the girls' bathrooms and found Laura's friend Sarah standing at the sink. She saw me in the mirror.

"Hey."

"Hey."

Seeing her gave me an idea. I'd hurt Laura with my lies, and we weren't speaking, but maybe I could still help her get to auditions with Sarah's help.

"Sarah?" She looked at me as she applied lip gloss. "I'm Laura's friend Zoe." Her eyes widened with recognition. "Or maybe I'm her former friend. After today I'm not sure." She didn't say anything. "Anyway, I have a favor to ask."

"Of me?" she questioned.

Was this the first time we'd spoken other than that time at Laura's sleepover? I thought it was, but I couldn't be sure. All my realities were starting to blur. "Yes." I stepped closer to the sink she was at. "I was hoping you could talk to Laura for me."

"Oh." She dropped her lip gloss back into her bag and

started to back away. "I don't get involved in other people's drama. Besides, I haven't spoken to her in forever."

"That's kind of what our fight was about," I said. "You see, after the sixth-grade play, I kind of told her you and your friends didn't like her." I could feel my face begin to warm.

Sarah pursed her lips. "Why would you say that?" she asked, sounding hurt. "It's not true. We couldn't understand why she suddenly ghosted us."

"I'm sorry. I thought you guys were taking her away from me, but the truth is, we were already growing apart. Now Laura is miserable, and I am too. She liked hanging out with you guys, and she should. Just like she should go to the drama club meeting."

"She's really good," Sarah agreed. "I kept telling her she should audition for a lead this year."

That made me feel worse. "She's not even going to the club meeting. At least, she wasn't planning on it this morning, but I know she's still here. She's probably at her locker. Do you think you could tell her to go with you? I know she'd listen."

Sarah seemed to think about it. "Okay," she said, and headed for the door.

I breathed a sigh of relief. Laura would go to the meeting. Maybe she'd sit with the drama queens and they'd all be friends again before the week was out. They could bond over what a terrible person I was. But at least I wouldn't mess up Laura's life like I'd messed up mine. "Oh, and Sarah?" She turned around again. "Don't tell her I asked you to do this. I wouldn't want her to change her mind and not go."

Sarah half smiled. "I won't. Thanks, Zoe."

So she did know my name.

By the time I left the bathroom, the halls had cleared. I looked to my right and saw Sarah talking to Laura, so I waited where I was till I saw the two of them disappear around a corner together. Whatever she had said worked. *Thanks, Sarah.* My stomach unclenched just slightly.

Next I made my way to the main office, which was still crowded. Walkie-talkies were being used to radio back and forth from the buses to the staff while secretaries took calls from parents who were either late to pickup or calling in a ride. No one noticed me standing at the main counter. Finally, a woman holding two phone receivers looked over.

"Can I use the phone?" I asked.

She waved her hand in the general direction of a phone on the counter. "Dial nine to get out."

"Thanks." The last time I'd been in here, I'd lost my phone. *Wait.* That gave me an idea. "Sorry. Excuse me! Hi! Sorry!" I waved my arms wildly to get the secretary's attention again, and when that didn't work, I pulled myself up partway onto the counter. "Do you know someone named Marge? She was working here yesterday?" Well, at least in the real world she had been. "I mean, today? Red hair? Dresses like it's 1955?" My heart swelled with hope as the woman seemed to think about this.

"Nope." She went back to the phone, picking up a new call. "Hello, Fairview Middle School. May I ask who is calling?"

I let myself drop back down to the ground. Marge was gone. My phone was dead. My life was ruined, and it was all my fault. My hands were shaking as I dialed my mom's number. She picked up on the first ring, probably because the caller ID said *the middle school.* "Mom? I'm fine—" I started to say.

"You should be at a club meeting!" Mom yelled. "Go! Go now! I don't care what kind of fight you had with Laura. You need to do something, Zoe. Get out there."

I held the receiver tighter. "You know about my fight with Laura?"

"You don't have to walk, but I can't get you till at least four," Mom continued, either not hearing me or not wanting to. "And why aren't you calling me from your own phone? You didn't break it, did you?"

"See you at four!" I said, and hung up fast.

Through the office windows, I could see the buses pulling away. The ringing phones started to die down, but that secretary was still staring at me. I guess she was wondering what I was still doing there. Finally, I walked out of the office and looked around. The halls were practically deserted. Did I try to find Ms. Pepper? I had no idea when Future City was starting again. I didn't even know what the other clubs were or what rooms they were in since I hadn't paid attention to the announcements. All I knew was I needed to avoid the drama department.

"Zoe! Hey!" Reagan came running down the hall, her backpack over one shoulder and a volleyball in her free hand. Jada was right behind her. "Are you coming to volleyball tryouts? They added another day because there are still some slots open. You should come!"

"Reagan, take a breath," Jada said, and gave me a look. "Hey. Are you all right? We heard what happened."

"*Maybe* heard," Reagan clarified. "Because I can't picture you ever pulling Laura's hair and screaming at her for posting a bad picture of you."

"I didn't do that, but we did have a fight," I admitted. "I don't really want to talk about it."

"I'm sorry," Jada said. "But if you need a boost, you should go read the positivity wall in the girls' bathroom. It's amazing." She hesitated. "Or you could just talk to us. I know we're not close," she said awkwardly, "but we are your friends."

Why had it taken me so long to realize that? These girls were my friends. I might not have had Laura, but Reagan and Jada had my back. "Thanks." I looked at my book bag instead of their faces. "It's complicated, but basically, it was my fault. I lied to Laura about something important, and she got mad." I attempted to smile and blink back tears. "But no one pulled anyone's hair. Do people even do that anymore?"

"On reality shows, yes," Reagan said knowingly.

"Especially *Thunder Shores*," Jada added.

"I love *Thunder Shores*." On the rare occasion Taryn watched TV with me, we always watched that because neither of us could ever believe what happened was real.

"That time Tabitha took Sasha's bikini and wore it to the juice bar without asking?" Reagan continues. "Major hair pulling in the vacation rental ensued."

"You didn't fight over her favorite bikini, did you?" Jada asked.

"No. Bikinis are sacred. I don't even own one. I think Laura does, though, and I'd never wear someone's bikini. That's kind of gross."

"Agreed," they both said.

Jada threw her arm around me, and one of her numerous beaded bracelets got tangled in my hair. "I've missed you! We never see you anymore since you quit volleyball and Future City. Clare said we have to get you back in the club."

I perked up. "Clare is on Future City now?" This was new!

"Yeah," Reagan said, looking at me strangely. "She joined last year when you were on it. She's team captain this year, and she's playing volleyball too. We see her all the time."

"That's amazing!" I said. "I wish I was still in the club."

"You can rejoin," Jada said. "And you can still make day two of volleyball tryouts. Come now!"

I hesitated. "I haven't practiced in months." Probably. If I'd quit, that had to be the case, and with the way my luck was going . . . "I probably wouldn't make the team at this point anyway."

"You won't with that attitude," Reagan said. "You still have today to wow them. What are you doing right now?"

"Absolutely nothing." I had an hour till Mom picked me up and zero people to hang out with. Well, that wasn't exactly true. Even though I'd obviously dropped Reagan and Jada because Laura had, they were still being as nice to me as they always were. We weren't best friends, but we were friends. I had been so distracted by Laura, that I hadn't bothered to see what was right under my nose the whole time. My eyes started to well up again.

"Hey." Reagan threw an arm around me now, and Jada sandwiched me on the other side. "No tears. You *will* make the team."

"That's not what I was—"

"Repeat after me!" Reagan sounded like a drill sergeant. Together, we made our way down the hallway. "I *will* make the team!"

"I *will* make the team!" I said as we turned down the

hall toward the gym. I could hear balls bouncing in the gym and people talking.

"Louder!"

I was starting to laugh, which seemed almost impossible considering how I'd felt just moments before. "I *will* make the team!"

"One more time with feeling!"

"I will make the team!" I shouted, and Reagan and Jada burst into applause.

"That's the spirit!" Reagan opened the gym door and motioned for me to go first.

"Heads-up!" someone shouted, but it was too late.

I took a volleyball to the face and hit the floor.

CHAPTER TWENTY-ONE

From far away I heard yelling and arguing.

"Zoe? Geez, is she okay? Zoe! Can you hear me?"

"What are you guys doing in here? You don't even play volleyball!"

"The gym was empty and the balls were there, so . . ."

"Dougie! You could have killed her."

"A lacrosse ball could have killed her. A volleyball will just cause a mild concussion. I think."

"A concussion? Someone needs to call her mom!"

"Find her phone. Check the bag! It's right there on the floor."

I heard rustling. "Found it! Hey. The phone is broken, and— Yowza, why is it so warm?"

"I heard Laura threw it at her head and it slammed into the wall."

"Dougie! Not true! Give me your phone."

"Use your own phone!"

I heard moaning. It took me a moment to realize it was coming from me.

"She's waking up. Zoe, hang on. We're calling your mom."

I sat up slowly. The room was sort of hazy before it slowly came into focus. There was a crowd of people around me.

"Hey." Clare's face appeared in front of me. "Welcome back. How do you feel?"

My hand went to my head. "Like I have a headache."

"Blame Dougie for throwing the ball!"

"Shut it, Jake."

"Should someone see if the nurse is still there?" Jake asked. "Zoe? Think you can stand up?"

"Yes." I tried to move on my own and stumbled. Everything around me was coming in and out of focus, like I was about to zip away, and yet I kept getting caught right where I was.

"I'll help you." Jake gave me an arm, and I leaned into him.

"You're nice. I see why Laura likes you."

"Laura likes him?" Dougie repeated. "Why is she always giving him looks to kill?"

"*Zoe.*" Jada's voice was a warning. "Stop talking."

"Because I made her think you liked someone else," I said, my words slurring slightly. "I'm a liar. A big fat liar who tried to keep doing retakes to change things, and it didn't work." Jake looked at me like I had three eyes.

"Okay, she's definitely got a concussion," Reagan said. "We need to find her mom."

"Mrs. Mitchell?" I heard Jada say. "It's Jada, Zoe's friend. She's fine, but she hit her head. Yes, she's okay. Yes, we're going to go to the nurse. Okay." She looked at us. "She's on her way."

"I'll meet her at the curb so she knows where to go," Reagan said.

"I'll get her to the nurse," Clare insisted, and helped me up and to the door. Jada was still talking to my mom. "You guys find Principal Higgins."

"Got it!" Dougie said, and jogged off with Jake down the hall. I could hear them talking as they ran. "Dude, Laura Lancaster likes you!"

"Are you okay to walk?" Clare asked me as I stumbled along. "I've got your phone in my pocket. It's broken, but I thought you'd want to have it with you when your mom came."

"Yeah." My head was throbbing, but at least my vision was clear again. This day just kept getting better. "I totally deserve this, you know. This is what happens when you try to trick your best friend into still liking you," I said mournfully. "Sorry. I shouldn't feel sorry for myself, not when it's my fault."

"What do you mean 'tricked'?" Clare asked. "You can't

trick someone into liking you. You had a fight. You'll make up."

This had to mean Clare didn't remember the app! If she did, she would have asked me about it. At least my retake for Clare had worked. I glanced her way. "Is that what happened with you and Ava?" I asked curiously. Clare looked at me strangely. "That's personal, sorry. But I heard you guys were close in elementary school."

"We were," Clare said, "but we grew apart. It hurt at first, but now I kind of think it was a good thing. We both found our people." She pushed a strand of teal hair behind her right ear. "Reagan and Jada are awesome, and Future City is the best club. You should come back."

I smiled through the pain. Clare seemed happy. At least I'd done something right. "I will." We hobbled a few more doors down to the nurse together. "Thanks, Clare."

"Of course!" she said, and helped me through the door. "And when you're feeling better, we should hang out." She grinned. "I have a feeling we'd get along."

"I do too," I agreed, and slowly sat down in a waiting room chair. Clare handed me my broken phone.

"Hello?" Clare called. "Is anyone still here?"

"What do we have here?"

I looked up. A woman with bright red hair and even redder glasses, wearing a blue sweater and a swishy skirt, was moving toward me. She had a huge string of pearls around her neck.

"Marge!" I cried, standing up fast. The room around me started to spin again, and I could hear a swooshing sound in my ears. "You're back! You can help me!"

Clare and Marge looked at each other.

"'Back'? Sweet pea, I've been here all afternoon." Marge led me to a cot. "The school nurse had to leave early to pick up her kid from the first day of school, so I'm holding down the fort. And of course I'm going to help you. I'm no doctor, but we can make you comfortable till your mother arrives."

I grabbed her arm and wouldn't let go. "It was you, wasn't it? You put the app on my phone!" I held up the cracked screen. Clare looked from me to Marge worriedly.

"Put what on your phone? Oh my, she's hysterical!" Marge got a cold compress from the refrigerator, cracked it, and placed it on my forehead. "Darling, you are not even making sense."

"I am too! I need you to fix my phone! I know you can," I begged.

"Darling, this isn't Verizon!" Marge chuckled.

"She was hit by a volleyball in the gym," Clare explained. "Her mom is on the way."

"I think she's in shock." Marge ushered Clare to the door. "Why don't you wait for her mother outside and bring her to the office for me? That's a good girl!" She closed the door behind her.

Marge put her hands on her hips and looked at me. "Why don't you just relax till your mother arrives?"

"I can't relax!" I insisted, feeling frustrated. I sat up fast, and the compress fell off my head and onto the floor. Marge bent down to pick it up. "My phone broke, and now I'm stuck here, and I've messed everything up. Nothing has gone right! I tried and tried to keep retaking all these moments, but every time I did something new, it only messed up my life more. I can't get back, and I've quit my favorite activities. I've ruined my friendships. I just wish I never tried to change anything. Well, except this one thing—I started the positivity wall in the bathroom, and I think it helped the girl who just left, so that was good."

Marge gave me back the ice pack. "I heard about that wall in the girls' bathroom. That's lovely."

"But everything else is a disaster. If I could just go back to the real first day of school, I wouldn't try to change a thing. I'd just let the year go wherever it was supposed to, whether it meant Laura and I were best friends or not. I get it now," I said, looking into her green eyes. "Things change and that's okay. I shouldn't use an app to stop it. Please." I held up my phone and showed her the cracked screen again. "Just get Retake off my phone. I know you were the one who put it on there when we met in the main office yesterday. I mean, *today*! Yesterday!" I held my head. "It feels like it's been on there for weeks."

"Sweet pea, just relax." Marge placed my hand with the phone down on the cot next to me.

"But . . ." I knew I should say more, but Marge's smile was sort of soothing.

"Stop talking," she said. "That's a good girl. Everything is going to work out just fine." She winked at me.

"Fine." That's the last word I heard before I saw the flash.

CHAPTER TWENTY-TWO

I woke up to the smell of pancakes, chocolate, and the sound of my alarm.

Beeeep! it blared, pushing me to get up. *Beeeep!* It sounded like it was coming from my . . . phone.

I sat up and looked over at my bedside table.

My phone! There it was, glowing softly without a scratch on it! I picked it up and looked at the date: September 7! It was the second day of school! I didn't have to do the first day over again! But was this my reality or an alternate one? There was only one way to be sure. I jumped out of bed and ran to my hamper. Taryn's white jeans with the brown stain were lying right on top. *Yes!* Heart pounding, I ran back to my bed and scrolled through my apps.

The bright pink icon was gone.

"DOUBLE YES!" I screamed, throwing myself back onto

my bed. (My old comforter and my stuffed animals were back too! Hello, Manny the Manatee!) I kicked my legs and pounded my fists as hard as I could and continued to scream so hard I thought I might cry.

I was back!

Thank you, Marge!

"OMG, would you stop screaming!" Taryn walked into my room holding her hairbrush. She only had makeup on her right eye. "And shut off your phone alarm. It's giving me a migraine."

I jumped out of bed and threw myself at her.

"What the . . . ?" Taryn just stood there as I clung to her midsection. "What is wrong with you?" Her voice was softer now. "The stain is going to come out of my jeans, I'm sure. And no one will even remember what happened yesterday. I promise."

"Who cares if they do?" I held on. I had my cranky, distant sister back and had never been happier to see her. I looked up at her. "Volleyball tryouts are still today, right?"

"Yes." Taryn looked at me strangely. "Didn't we just talk about this yesterday afternoon? I told you I spoke to the coach for you. You better be there."

"I won't miss them," I said, feeling practically giddy. "Even if I don't make the team, I'm going to at least show up and try out."

"Okay, good." Taryn narrowed her eyes. "I don't want to

hear this garbage that because Laura isn't trying out, you aren't trying out."

"I'm not," I promised. "I don't care what Laura does. I mean, I care, and I wish she were doing volleyball, too, but there is no way I'm not trying out for the team. I like volleyball too much. And I love Future City and am doing that too! With Reagan, Jada, and this girl Clare. She's awesome." I was aware I was talking really fast. "I'm not sure why I've never hung out with her before. But I will now. We should hang out more too. I miss you, and I could really use some help doing this whole seventh-grade thing. As the white jeans have taught me, I don't have a clue about anything."

There. I said it. I put myself out there. If the Retake app had taught me one thing, it was that the past was in the past for a reason. I'd always have my memories of me and Laura, but there was no need to try to redo them. It was time to look forward and make new memories. That's what seventh grade was all about.

Taryn put her hand to my forehead. "Maybe you really do have a fever."

I pushed her hand away. "I don't have a fever. I just miss you. I know you have your own friends and a life that is way cooler than mine, but I miss you, Taryn Golightly."

Taryn grinned. "You haven't used that name for me in years."

"Because we haven't watched Audrey together in years! And I could use some more Audrey."

"So could I," Taryn said with a sigh, and looked at me. "Okay, I'm not committing to Saturday night because that's when I'm usually out."

"Of course."

"But Friday night would work for some sisterly bonding. *If* you really miss it."

"I miss it! I miss us!"

"Really?" Taryn looked at me with interest. "I'd kind of gotten the impression that Laura was like the sister you always wanted and you didn't need me anymore."

I hugged her again. "Not true. I definitely need you. Especially now! And Audrey."

"Everyone needs Audrey," Taryn agreed, and we both smiled. She held up her hairbrush. "I have to finish my hair before the bus comes, but if you want, I'll help you find something to wear." She raised her right eyebrow. "I may even let you borrow something from my closet since we don't want you repeating the white jeans–isode from yesterday." We both laughed. Taryn headed to my closet.

"Definitely not," I said, and ran over to grab my phone. I quickly texted Reagan and Jada.

Me: Hey! See you at the bus! Save me a seat with you guys!

A reply came right back.

Jada: Always! See you soon.

Reagan: Don't wear white jeans! LOL

Me: I'm not! My sister is picking my outfit!

"How about this?" I heard Taryn say, and I headed over to my closet. She was holding up a navy tank top with tiny blue pom-pom fringe that I recognized. My closet was also back to normal and a complete disaster. I would have to do something about that.

"I like it," I said. "Can I wear it with jeans? *Blue* jeans?"

"Yes." Taryn's head was still in my closet. "Let me just see which sandals you have that will go best with it. Go with flats. You won't trip. This one time I wore cork wedges in middle school, and I tripped over someone's foot and went flying."

As Taryn talked, my eyes landed on the corkboard over my desk. I moved in closer to look at the pictures. All of my original photos were back. I stared at one of Laura and me in the tree house, taken before the summer. A Jenga tower was built in front of us, and our sleeping bags were curled up behind us.

Taryn stood beside me. "She's a jerk." No name was needed.

"She's not," I said, lifting the picture off the corkboard. We both stared at it. "I mean, she didn't have to just ditch me like she did, but it's time to move on. We want to do different things."

I wasn't going to lie: It still hurt. I didn't get why Laura couldn't be friends with me and with the drama queens, but I couldn't turn myself into who she wanted me to be just to make her happy, and she couldn't keep doing what I liked to make me happy. Like Mom said, Laura's and my friendship fading didn't necessarily mean it was over. Maybe it just meant it would change again and again, like friendships do.

"You sound like Mom," Taryn said.

"She's right, but don't tell her I said that." I started to take down the rest of the pictures of Laura and me. Taryn quietly helped me. I wouldn't throw them out. I'd just stick them in a drawer to remember later. The pictures and the memories were real. Unlike some of our posts on social media, they hadn't been posed. And no matter what happened, these memories couldn't be erased.

Well, except for maybe in the retake. And I was definitely never looking for that again. I didn't need a retake. Seventh grade was going to be just fine without one.

"Girls! It's not summer anymore! Get a move on!" Mom called up the stairs, and Taryn threw me the tank top.

It was time for school.

Mom was waiting at the bottom of the stairs with my lunch. "Now, the bus is going to be fine, I'm sure, and you already printed out your schedule again, right?"

I paused on the bottom step. "I know it now." I was technically on day four of classes. "And the bus is fine. Jada and Reagan are saving me a seat. I'm going to go to volleyball tryouts with them after school, and I think Future City starts next week."

Mom smiled. "Thatta girl."

"But keep your phone on," I added as I kissed her cheek and headed out the door. "Just in case someone hits me in the face with a ball."

"What?"

"Bye, Taryn!" I shouted up the stairs.

"Bye!" she called back.

Waiting at the bus stop, I couldn't help myself: I still clicked on Instagram. The picture of Laura and the drama queens at Ava's pool was waiting. The five of them were posing on a rock ledge with a waterfall behind them, and every single one of them had something green on. I read Laura's hashtag: #summerlastsforeverwfriends!

This time, I didn't let myself get upset over it. Instead, I clicked like. Why not? We were still friends. Then I kept scrolling, looking for the feed of my favorite German soccer player. Then I found a Girls Who Look Like Hepburn group and followed that. Some of the girls really did look like Audrey. Or maybe they really didn't. With filters and editing, pictures could be anything you wanted them to be. Trying to retake a picture to make my life seem better was ridiculous. That picture was just a teeny-tiny snapshot of one minuscule second of someone's day. And who knew what it even took to get that picture right? If it was anything like what happened when Mom tried to get a decent picture of Taryn and me together on vacation, I knew it took about three dozen attempts before there was a good one of us smiling.

I slipped my phone into my bag. It was time to concentrate on living my life, not staging the perfect picture.

The bus pulled up, and I stepped on. I spotted Reagan and Jada right away.

"I like your top!" Jada said. "Where did you get it? Blue looks good on you. Did you print your schedule?"

"Jada!" Reagan said. "Chill." We all started to laugh. "Sorry. Second-day jitters. Yesterday was hard."

"It was," I agreed. I'd had a lot of hard days lately, but I could already tell today wasn't going to be one of them. "But at least we're together. Are you guys around this weekend? Maybe we could have a sleepover at my house. I have this awesome tree house."

Reagan and Jada looked at each other. "I have always wanted to see your tree house. The pictures you and Laura have posted of it look so cool."

"Well, there are lots of bugs, but we have twinkle lights and the Wi-Fi works up there, so we can bring a speaker," I said.

"Will Laura come too?" Jada asked awkwardly.

"I don't think so," I said, and left it at that. "But we can ask Clare."

Jada smiled. "I like Clare. She always has the best ideas at Future City. Let's."

We spent the rest of the bus ride thinking of games we'd play. Reagan had some dice game called Tenzi, and Jada swore she had her own recipe for mud masks that we had to try. Reagan looked a little nervous about that, but I was already looking forward to the weekend ahead instead of looking back.

When the bus pulled up at school, Clare was just stepping off her bus as well. Today she had on a female Thor graphic tee; jeans she'd obviously doctored herself with hearts, words, and emojis; and beat-up tennis shoes. "Hey! So, Zoe, do you need to stop at the main office again for your schedule?"

"Nope." I smiled at her. "I've memorized it by now."

Clare grinned. "It's about time."

"Hey. Want to have sleepover with us this weekend?" I asked. "In my tree house?"

"I'm in," Clare said. "Let's do a séance."

"A séance?" Jada squeaked.

"Those are fake, right?" Reagan added, laughing nervously.

"Maybe, but they're fun." Clare shrugged as we walked into school together.

When we parted ways with Reagan and Jada at the stairs, I spotted the nurse's office out of the corner of my eye.

"Give me one second," I told Clare. I hurried into the office. The phone was ringing off the hook, and a young nurse looked frazzled. "Excuse me, I said. "Is there a Marge Simpkins working today? Or in the main office? She was here yesterday afternoon. I think she's a temp."

The nurse frowned. "We don't have temps in the nurse's office."

"Redhead? Dresses very vintage?" I added, feeling my stomach drop. "Red glasses?"

"Nope." The nurse glared at the phone still ringing. "Are you feeling okay? Otherwise, I really need to get that phone."

"I'm fine now." I looked around.

She'd been here, hadn't she? I couldn't help but smile and wonder.

———

The second day of school went fine. I didn't get lost. I didn't forget my schedule, and I didn't get hit with a ball. I did, however, use the girls' bathroom on the second floor with Clare and found the positivity wall was still there. Girls were already adding to the messages and creating new ones. I was glad to see that one of my retakes had worked out.

I sat with Clare, Reagan, and Jada at lunch, and we talked about *Thunder Shores* for almost thirty minutes. Jada laughed so hard at Clare's impression of Beverly, the most popular character, that Gatorade came out of her nose.

"Did anyone see?" she kept asking as we walked out of the cafeteria.

I looked around. I saw Dougie, Shardul, and Jake at one table, and Laura and her new friends at the table beside it. No one was looking our way. "I think you're safe," I said as we walked out.

But when I stopped to throw out my lunch bag, I felt someone's eyes on me. I turned around.

It was Laura. We stared at each other across the crowded cafeteria. Finally, I gave a little wave. Laura waved back.

It wasn't much, but it was enough.

On my way home on the bus, I talked with Reagan and Jada for a while; then I pulled out my phone and clicked on Instagram. This time I took a selfie right there on the bus and hashtagged it #seconddayof7. I thought for a few minutes about what I wanted to write.

First day was the worst, I wrote, *but second day is looking up. Anyone else get completely lost everywhere they went yesterday?* Then I changed my hashtag to #bemorereal #fairviewms and clicked share. I spent the next few minutes scrolling through my feed. The German soccer player seemed to be eating a lot of gelato in Italy this week. Suddenly I saw the alert. My post not only had likes, it had

tons of comments, and from people I didn't even know followed me.

> **dougdman:** Dude, got stuck in locker room for ten
> minutes looking for way out!
> **candykisses:** Sat in wrong French class and had no
> clue. #firstdayworstday
> **mara8late:** Every teacher pronounced my name
> wrong.
> **marisolp:** Couldn't open locker. Had to carry books
> all day.

Marisol was commenting on my posts? I couldn't believe it. The comments kept going. It seemed like anyone
and everyone I knew and didn't know at Fairview had
tons of comments about the first day of school. I scrolled
through them and saw a familiar handle.

> **lauraslitlife:** ♥

It was always simply a heart emoji, but it was there, just
like our friendship would be in some way.

The important thing was that I wasn't alone. I smiled
and slipped my phone back into my pocket. Then I put my
head back and enjoyed the ride.

ACKNOWLEDGMENTS

I wouldn't be writing this "thank you" if it weren't for a fateful afternoon spent talking books with Beverly Horowitz and Kelsey Horton. Thank you both for welcoming me to the Delacorte Press/Random House family and for letting me sink my teeth into a project that I love so fiercely. Kelsey, I couldn't have asked for a better editor on this project. You helped me keep track of Zoe's past, present, and future, and I couldn't have done it without you. Special thanks also goes to the rest of the Delacorte team, including Michelle Cunningham, for the beautiful book design; Alexandra Hess; and Colleen Fellingham.

Dan Mandel, thank you for being such a great partner in everything I do. And to Elizabeth Eulberg, Kieran Viola, Sarah Mlynowski, Jennifer E. Smith, Tiffany Schmitt, and Lindsay Currie for always being my sounding board.

Finally to my family—Mike, Tyler, Dylan, Jack and Ben—I'd never want another retake with this crew. Thank you for being my everything.

ABOUT THE AUTHOR

Jen Calonita is the author of the award-winning Fairy Tale Reform School series and *Secrets of My Hollywood Life,* as well as *Conceal, Don't Feel,* and *Mirror, Mirror* in the Twisted Tale series. She lives in New York with her husband, two boys, and two Chihuahuas named Captain Jack Sparrow and Ben Kenobi.

jencalonitaonline.com